The Mist

The Mist

RAGNAR JÓNASSON

Translated from the Icelandic
by Victoria Cribb

MINOTAUR
BOOKS
NEW YORK

First published in the United States by Minotaur Books, an imprint of St. Martin's Publishing Group

THE MIST. Copyright © 2017 by Ragnar Jónasson. English translation copyright © 2020 by Victoria Cribb. All rights reserved. Printed in the United States of America. For information, address St. Martin's Publishing Group, 120 Broadway, New York, NY 10271.

www.minotaurbooks.com

The Library of Congress Cataloging-in-Publication Data is available upon request.

ISBN 978-1-250-76811-7 (hardcover)
ISBN 978-1-250-76812-4 (ebook)

Our books may be purchased in bulk for promotional, educational, or business use. Please contact your local bookseller or the Macmillan Corporate and Premium Sales Department at 1-800-221-7945, extension 5442, or by email at MacmillanSpecialMarkets@macmillan.com.

Originally published in Iceland under the title *Mistur* by Veröld Publishing

First published in Great Britain by Michael Joseph, an imprint of Penguin Books, a Penguin Random House company

First U.S. Edition: 2020

10 9 8 7 6 5 4 3 2 1

To Kira and Natalía

Special thanks to Hulda María Stefánsdóttir for her advice on police procedure.

Fond thanks also to my parents, Jónas Ragnarsson and Katrín Guðjónsdóttir, for reading the manuscript.

'The days passed slowly
but the years flew by
and still I kept talking to you in my emptiness.'

– Ólafur Jóhann Ólafsson, *The Almanac* (2015)
(Trans. Ólafur Jóhann Ólafsson)

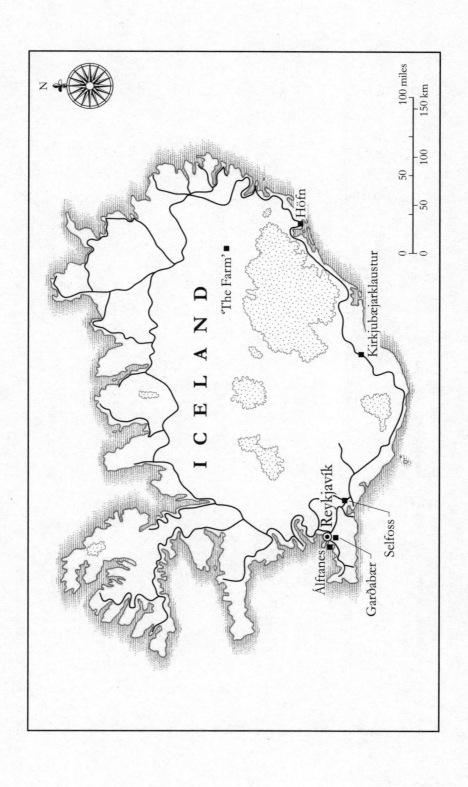

The Mist

Prologue

February 1988

Hulda Hermannsdóttir opened her eyes.

So heavy and unrelenting was the sense of lethargy weighing her down that she felt as if she'd been drugged. She could have gone on sleeping all day, even here in her hard chair. It was just as well that, as a detective, she merited an office to herself. It meant she could shut the door on the outside world and wait for the hours to pass, either by staring into space or letting her eyelids droop. Meanwhile, the documents piled up on the desk in front of her. Since returning from leave two weeks ago she hadn't got to grips with a single case.

This neglect hadn't gone entirely unnoticed by her boss, Snorri, although, to his credit, he was treating her with patient understanding. The fact was she'd simply had to come back to work; she couldn't bear to spend another minute cooped up in the house with Jón. Even the breathtaking natural beauty of their home on Álftanes couldn't work its magic on her these days. She was deaf to the sighing of the waves and blind to the stars and Northern Lights shimmering across the sky. She and Jón hardly spoke to each other, and she'd given up initiating any conversations with him, although she still answered if he addressed her directly.

The February darkness did nothing to help. It was the coldest, greyest time of the year, and every new day seemed to bring a deterioration in the weather. As if things weren't bad enough, the snow had been coming down heavily that month, burying the city in a muffling layer and clogging its arteries. Cars kept getting stuck in the streets, and it took all Hulda's skill to navigate the unploughed back roads of Álftanes in her Skoda, despite its regulation studded tyres, before making it safely on to the main road at Kópavogur.

For a while she had doubted she would ever return to work. In fact, she'd doubted she would ever leave the house again, or find the strength to crawl out from under her duvet. But in the end there were only two options: to stay at home with Jón or sit in her office from dawn to dusk, even if she achieved little in the way of work.

Having opted for the office, she struggled to concentrate and instead spent her days moving files and reports from one pile to another, trying to read them but feeling unable to focus. Things couldn't go on like this, she reasoned; they had to get better. Of course, she would never get over her guilt – she knew that – but the pain would inevitably be blunted over time. At least she could cling to that hope. But for now her anger towards Jón, far from dissipating, was growing and festering. With every day that passed she could sense the rage and hatred churning ever more corrosively inside her, and she knew that it wasn't doing her any good, but she just couldn't control her emotions. She had to find an outlet for them somehow . . .

When the phone rang on her desk, Hulda didn't react. Lost in a dark, private world, she didn't even raise her eyes until it had rung several times. Then, at last, moving sluggishly, as if under water, she picked up the receiver. 'Hulda.'

'Hello, Hulda. Snorri here.'

She immediately felt unsettled. Her boss didn't usually ring her unless it was urgent. Their contact was normally limited to morning meetings, and he didn't, as a rule, interfere much in the day-to-day handling of her investigations.

'Oh, hello,' she said after a slight delay.

'Could you pop in and see me? Something's come up.'

'I'm on my way.' She put down the receiver, rose to her feet and checked her appearance in the small mirror she kept in her handbag. However awful she felt, she was determined not to show any sign of weakness at work. Of course, none of her colleagues could be in any doubt of the state she was in, but what she dreaded more than anything was being sent on compassionate leave again. The only way to hang on to the shreds of her sanity was to keep herself busy.

Snorri greeted her with a smile as she stepped into his office, which was so much larger than her own. Feeling the waves of sympathy emanating from him, she cursed under her breath, afraid any show of kindness from him would undermine her hard-won self-control.

'How are you, Hulda?' he asked, waving her to a seat before she had a chance to reply.

'Fine, fine, under the circumstances.'

'How are you finding being back in the office?'

'I'm just getting into gear again. Tying up the loose ends on some of last year's cases. It's all coming along.'

'Are you absolutely sure you're up to it?' Snorri asked. 'I'm perfectly happy to grant you more time off, should you need it. Of course, *we* need you here too, as you know, but we want to be sure you're up to coping with the more challenging cases.'

'I can understand that.'

'And are you?'

'Am I what?'

'Up to coping?'

'Yes,' she lied, looking him straight in the eye.

'Right, well. In that case, something's come up and I'd like you to look into it, Hulda.'

'Oh?'

'An ugly business.' He paused before frowning and emphasizing his words with a wave of his arm: '*Bloody* ugly, in fact. Suspected murder out east. We need to send someone over there right now. I'm so sorry to spring this on you so soon after your return, but no one else with your experience is free at the moment.'

Hulda thought he could have done a better job of dressing this up as a compliment, but never mind.

'Of course I can go. I'm perfectly up to it,' she replied, aware even as she said it that this was a lie. 'Whereabouts in the east?'

'Oh, some farmhouse miles from anywhere. It's unbeliev-able anyone's still making a go of farming out there.'

'Who's the victim? Do we know yet?'

'The victim? Oh, sorry, Hulda, I didn't give you the full story. We're not just talking about one body . . .' He paused. 'Apparently, the discovery was pretty horrific. It's not clear how long the bodies have been lying there, but they're guessing since Christmas at least . . .'

PART ONE

Two months earlier –
just before Christmas 1987

I

The end.

Erla put down her book and leaned back in the shabby old armchair with a deep sigh.

She had no idea of the time. The grandfather clock in the sitting room had stopped working a while ago – in fact, it must be several years ago now. They had no idea how to mend it themselves and it was so heavy and unwieldy that they had never seriously considered lugging it out to the old jeep and driving it down the long, bumpy road to the village. They couldn't even be sure it would fit in the car or that anyone in the village would have the necessary skills to repair such an antique mechanism. So it was left where it was, reduced to the status of an ornament. The clock had belonged to her husband Einar's grandfather. The story was that he had brought it back with him from Denmark, where he had gone to attend agricultural college before returning home to take over the farm. It was what had been expected of him, as Einar used to say. Later, it had been his father's turn,

9

before finally the baton had passed on to Einar himself. His grandfather was long dead; his father too, somewhat before his time. Farming out here, even just living out here, took its mental and physical toll.

She became aware that it was freezing cold. Of course, that was to be expected at this time of year. The house was feeling its age and when the wind blew from a certain quarter the only way to keep warm in some of the rooms, like here in the sitting room, was to wrap yourself in a thick blanket, as she had done now. The blanket kept her body snug, but her hands, sticking out from under it, were so chilly that it was hard to turn the pages. Still, she put up with it. Reading gave her greater pleasure than anything else she knew. A good book could transport her far, far away, to a different world, another country, another culture, where the climate was warmer and life was easier. That's not to imply that she was ungrateful or discontented with the farm or its location, not really. It was Einar's family home, after all, so the only thing for it was to grit one's teeth and make the best of it. Growing up in post-war Reykjavík, Erla had never dreamt of becoming a farmer's wife in the wild Icelandic highlands, but when she met Einar he had swept her off her feet. Then, when they were still in their early twenties, Anna had come along.

She thought about Anna, whose house was in a rather better state than theirs. It had been built much more recently, at a little distance from their place, originally as accommodation for tenant farmers. The worst part about the distance was that they couldn't easily pop round to see each other when the weather closed in like this, or at least only with considerable difficulty. Einar usually parked up the jeep over the harshest winter months, since even with the four-wheel drive, nailed tyres and chains were little use when the snow really started coming down, day after day after day. In those conditions, it was easier to get around on foot or on cross-country skis, so it was fortunate that both she and Einar were quite competent skiers. It would have been fun to have had the chance to go skiing more often – even if only a handful of times – to try out their skills on proper downhill slopes, but there had never been much time for that sort of thing. Money had always been tight too; the farm just about broke even, but they couldn't justify spending much on leisure pursuits or travelling. They rarely discussed it. The goal now, as ever, was to keep their heads above water, keep the farm going, and in the black, if possible. For Einar, she knew, the honour of the family was at stake; he had shouldered a heavy ancestral burden and his forefathers were like an unseen presence, forever watching him from the wings.

His grandfather, Einar Einarsson the first, kept an eye on them in the oldest part of the house, where Erla was sitting now; the original timber structure that he had built 'with his own two hands, with blood, sweat and tears', as her husband had once put it. Einar's father, Einar Einarsson the second, presided over what Erla referred to as the new wing, the concrete extension that now housed the bedrooms and had been built when her husband, Einar Einarsson the third, was a child.

Erla didn't feel anything like the same reverence for

her own forebears. She seldom spoke of them. Her parents, who were divorced, lived down south, and she hardly ever saw her three sisters. Of course, distance played a part, but the truth was that her family had never been that close. After her parents split up, her sisters had stopped making much effort to stay in touch, and family get-togethers were few and far between. Erla didn't shed many tears over the fact. It would have been nice to have her own support network to fall back on, but she had become a member of Einar's family instead and focused on cultivating a relationship with them.

She didn't stir from her chair. She didn't have the energy to get up quite yet. After all, there was nowhere to go but to bed, and she wanted to stay awake a little longer, savouring the peace and quiet. Einar had fallen asleep hours ago. To him, rising early was a virtue and, anyway, he had to feed the sheep. But at this time of year, just before Christmas, with the day at its shortest, Erla could see no earthly reason to drag herself out of bed first thing, while it was still pitch dark. It wouldn't even start to get light until around eleven and, in her opinion, that was quite early enough to wake up in December. Over the years, the couple had learned not to quarrel over such trivial differences as when to get out of bed. It wasn't as if they received many visitors out here, so they had no choice but to get on with each other. They still loved each other too, perhaps not like in the old days when they had first met, but their love had matured as their relationship deepened.

Erla rather regretted having devoured the book so fast; she should have spun it out a little longer. Last time they drove to the village together she had borrowed fifteen novels from the library, which was over the limit, of course, but she had a special arrangement, as was only natural in the circumstances. She was allowed to keep the books out on loan for longer than usual too, sometimes for as long as two or three months, when the weather was at its worst. Now, though, she had read all fifteen; this had been the last one. She had finished them unusually quickly, although God only knew when she would next make it to the library. It would have been unfair to ask Einar to fetch more books when he skied to the village the other day, as they would only have weighed him down. She was overwhelmed by the familiar feeling of emptiness that assailed her whenever something ran out and she knew she had no chance of replacing it. She was stranded here. To describe the feeling as emptiness didn't really do it justice; it would be truer to say she felt almost like a prisoner up here in the wilderness.

All talk of claustrophobia was forbidden on the farm, though; it was a feeling they had to ignore, because otherwise it could so easily have become unbearable.

Suffocating . . .

Yes, it had been a really good book, the best of the fifteen. But not so good that she could face rereading it straight away. And she'd read all their other books, the ones they'd either bought or inherited with the house; some of them over and over again.

Her gaze fell on the fir tree standing in the corner of the sitting room. For once, Einar had put some effort into selecting a handsome specimen. The aromatic scent filling the little room was a cosy reminder that Christmas was coming. They always did their best to banish the darkness, however briefly, during the festive season, converting their loneliness into a welcome solitude. Erla relished the thought that during this season of peace and rest from their labours they would be left completely alone, quite literally, because no one would ever make it this far inland in the snow, unless they were unusually determined. And so far, that had never happened.

The tree hadn't been decorated yet. It was a family tradition to do it on 23 December, St Thorlákur's Mass, but there were already a few parcels arranged underneath it. There was no point trying to hide the presents from each other, as they had all been bought ages ago. After all, it wasn't as though they could run out to the shops on Christmas Eve to buy any items they'd forgotten, like last-minute gifts or cream for the gravy.

There were books under the tree, she knew that for sure, and it was awfully tempting to open one early. Einar always gave her at least a couple of novels, and the thing she looked forward to more than anything else at Christmas was discovering what they were, then settling down in the armchair with a box of chocolates and a traditional drink of malt brew to read late into the night. All the preparations had been done. The box of chocolates was lying unopened on the dining table. The malt and orange brew was in the larder and no one was allowed to touch it until the festivities officially started, which, according to Icelandic tradition, was at 6 p.m. on the twenty-fourth, when the bells rang for the Christmas Mass. It went without saying that they would be having the customary dish of smoked lamb, or *hangikjöt*, for their main Christmas dinner on the evening of the twenty-fourth. Like last year, and the year before that; like every year . . .

Erla stood up, a little stiffly, feeling the chill striking into her flesh the moment she emerged from her warm cocoon. Going over to the sitting-room window, she drew back the curtain and peered out into the darkness. It was snowing. But then she knew that. It always snowed here in winter. What else could she expect in Iceland, living so far inland, so high above sea level? She smiled a little wryly: this was no place for people, not at this time of year. The stubbornness of Einar's ancestors was admirable in its way, but now Erla felt as if she were being punished for their decisions. Thanks to them, she was stuck here.

The farm had to be kept going, whatever the cost. Not that she meant to complain – of course not. Several farms in the neighbourhood – if she could call such a wide, sparsely populated area a neighbourhood – had been abandoned in the last decade, and Einar's reaction was always the same: he cursed those who moved away for their cowardice in giving up so easily. And, anyway, if they gave up the farm, what would they do for a living? They couldn't be sure the land would be worth anything if they tried to sell it, and other job opportunities were thin on the ground out here. She simply couldn't imagine Einar wanting to work for somebody else after being his own master for most of his life.

'Erla,' she heard him calling from the bedroom, his

voice hoarse. She was sure she'd heard him snoring earlier. 'Why don't you come to bed?'

'I'm on my way,' she said, and switched off the lamp in the sitting room, then blew out the candle she'd lit on the table beside her to create a cosy atmosphere while she was reading.

Einar had turned on his light. He was lying on his side of the bed, ever the creature of habit: the glass of water, alarm clock and Laxness novel on the nightstand. Erla knew him well enough to realize he felt it looked good to have a classic like Laxness by the bed, though in practice he never made much headway with it in the evenings. They owned most of Halldór Laxness's works and she had read and reread them herself, but what Einar really looked at these days were old newspapers and magazines, or articles about the paranormal. Of course, their newspapers were always out of date, some much more so than others: at this time of year, months could pass between papers. Nevertheless, they kept up their subscription to the party mouthpiece, copies of which piled up at the post office in between their visits there, and to several periodicals as well, like the Icelandic *Reader's Digest*.

Although Einar's interest in current affairs was perfectly understandable, she couldn't for the life of her see the attraction of ghost stories or books by psychics about the spirit world, not when they lived in an eerie place like this.

In winter, not a day passed when she didn't witness something that sent a shiver down her spine. She didn't believe in ghosts, but the isolation, the silence, the damned darkness, they all combined to amplify every creak of the floorboards and walls, the moaning of the wind, the flicker of light and shadow, to the extent that she sometimes wondered if maybe she should believe in ghosts after all; if maybe that would make life more bearable.

It was only when she sat reading a book by candlelight, immersed in an unfamiliar world, that the phantoms in her head lost all their power to frighten her.

Erla climbed into bed and searched for a comfortable position. She tried to look forward to the morning, but it wasn't easy. She wanted to be as enchanted by this place – by the solitude – as Einar was, but she just couldn't make herself feel it, not any more. She knew that tomorrow would be no better, that it wouldn't be very different from the day which had just ended. Christmas brought a slight variation in their routine, but that was all. New Year's Eve was just another day too, though they always had a special meal then as well, smoked lamb, like on Christmas Eve, but they hadn't let off any fireworks for donkey's years. Since fireworks counted as hazardous items, they were on sale only for a limited period, which meant they were never available when she and Einar made their pre-Christmas trip to the village to stock up. This was usually in November, before the worst of the snow set in, and it would be hard to justify making another special trip in the depths of winter, just to buy a few rockets and sparklers. Besides, they both agreed that letting off fireworks in the middle of nowhere was a bit pointless. At least, that's how Einar had put it, and she had humoured him as usual, though in her heart of hearts she missed the explosion of colour with which they used to greet the New Year.

'Why are you up so late, love?' he asked gently.

She saw from her alarm clock that it wasn't even eleven, but here in this perpetual darkness, time had little meaning. They lived according to their own rhythm, going to bed far too early, waking up far too early. Her silent rebellion, which consisted of staying up reading, didn't achieve anything.

'I was finishing my book,' she said. 'I just wasn't sleepy. And I was wondering if we should ring Anna to see if she's all right.' Answering her own question, she added: 'But it's probably too late to call now.'

'Can I turn off the light?' he asked.

'Yes, do,' she said reluctantly. He pressed the switch and they were engulfed by darkness. So uncompromising, yet so quiet. Not the faintest light to be seen. She could *feel* the snow coming down outside; knew that they wouldn't be going anywhere soon. This was the life they had made for themselves. There was nothing to be done but endure it.

II

It was long past 10 p.m. Hulda was standing outside the front door, fumbling in her bag for the house keys and cursing under her breath. She couldn't see a thing. The light bulb over the door had blown and the glow of the streetlights was too faint to be much help.

Jón had promised to buy a new bulb but, clearly, he hadn't got round to it yet. They were half in the country-side out here by the sea on the Álftanes peninsula, away from the bright lights of the city. She had always thought of it as a good place to live, yet a sense of gloom had been hanging over the family for the last few months, as if their skies were overcast.

Hulda found her keys at last. She hadn't wanted to ring the bell in case Jón and Dimma were asleep. She had been expecting to get home even later since she was supposed to be on night shift, but for once things had been quiet, so Snorri had let her go early. He was quite perceptive, she'd give him that, and could probably sense that all was not well at home. She and her husband, Jón, both worked too hard, and their hours were far from conventional. Jón was a self-employed investor and wholesaler, and although that should theoretically have given him considerable control over his time, in practice he spent long hours closeted in his study at home or at meetings in town. Whenever there was a lot on, Hulda was expected to do overtime, and she had to do evenings and nights when required, as well as still working the odd holiday. This year, for example, she was down to be on duty on Christmas Day. With any luck, there would be nothing to do, though, and she'd be home at a reasonable hour.

All was quiet in the house. The lights were off in the sitting room and the kitchen, and Hulda immediately noticed that there was no lingering smell of food. It seemed that yet again Jón hadn't bothered to cook dinner for himself and their daughter. He was supposed to make sure Dimma was fed; she couldn't live on Cheerios alone for breakfast and supper. It wouldn't help her mood if she never got a square meal, and she had been difficult enough recently as it was. She was thirteen, and her teens hadn't got off to a good start. She had been neglecting her schoolfriends and spending her evenings alone at home, shut away in her room. Hulda had always assumed that Álftanes would be a wonderful place to bring up a child, a good mix of city and countryside, reasonably close to Reykjavík but with the great outdoors on their doorstep, and plenty of clean, healthy sea air. Now, though, she had to admit that the decision to live here might have been a mistake: perhaps they should have moved closer to the centre of town, to give their daughter more of a social life.

Hulda was standing in the hall when Dimma's door unexpectedly opened and Jón came out.

'Back already?' he asked, meeting her gaze with a smile. 'So early? I thought I'd have to stay up late to have a chance of seeing you.'

'What were you doing in Dimma's room? Is she asleep?'

'Yes, sound asleep. I was just checking on her. She seemed so under the weather this evening. I just wanted to make sure she was OK.'

'Oh? Has she got a temperature?'

'No, nothing like that. Her forehead feels quite cool. I think it's best to let her sleep. She seems so down in the dumps at the moment.'

Jón came over, put his arm round Hulda and more or less walked her into the sitting room. 'Why don't we have a glass of wine, love? I went to the *Ríki* today and bought two bottles of red.'

Hulda hesitated, still worried about Dimma. Something didn't feel quite right, but she pushed the thought away. The fact was, she needed to unwind after a tiring day at work; her job took it out of her enough as it was, without her having to be on edge at home as well. Perhaps Jón was right, perhaps she just needed a drink to help her relax before bed.

She took off her coat, laid it over the back of the sofa and sat down. Jón went into the kitchen and returned with a bottle and two antique glasses that had belonged to her grandparents. He pulled out the cork with an effort and filled them. This was an unusual luxury. Not only was the tax on alcohol prohibitive, but it was hard for either of them to make it to the *Ríki*, as the state-owned off-licence was known, during its restricted opening hours.

'Red wine! We're very extravagant all of a sudden. What are we celebrating?'

'The fact I've had a good day,' he said. 'I think I've finally managed to sell that building on Hverfisgata that I've been struggling to shift. The bank's been on my back, threatening to repossess it. Bunch of bloody bean counters, the lot of them – they have no idea how business works. Anyhow, cheers!'

'Cheers.'

'There are times when I really wish we lived abroad, somewhere with proper banks. It's so frustrating trying to work in an environment where everything comes down to politics, and the banks are all run by former politicians too. It's crazy. I'm in the wrong party and I'm being made to suffer for the fact.' He gave an aggrieved sigh.

Hulda only listened with half an ear. She hadn't the patience to keep up with all the ins and outs of Jón's endless financial entanglements. She had enough problems of her own at work but made it a strict policy not to bring them home, as he was inclined to do. She had every confidence in his skill at wheeling and dealing; he seemed to know all the tricks. One minute he was buying a prime piece of property, next thing she knew he'd sold it for a hefty profit, and the rest of the time he was busy building up his wholesale business. She had to hand it to him, he had certainly secured them a comfortable income over the years. They owned this attractive detached house, two cars and could afford to treat themselves to the odd luxury as well, like taking Dimma out to dinner once or twice a month, usually at their favourite hamburger joint. Reykjavík, only ten minutes away by car, had so few restaurants that even going to a fast-food place counted as a special occasion. Come to think of it, it was quite a while since they'd last been for a meal as a family. Dimma seemed to have grown out of wanting to spend time with her parents and had refused several invitations to come out with them in the last few weeks and months.

'Jón, why don't we go out for a meal tomorrow?'

'On Thorlákur's Mass? Everywhere's bound to be heaving.'

'I was just thinking about our usual place, about going for a burger and chips.'

'Hm . . .' After a brief pause, he said: 'Let's wait and see. It's bound to be packed and the rush-hour traffic's always so bad this close to Christmas. Don't forget we still need to decorate the tree too.'

'Oh, damn,' she said. 'I forgot to pick one up today.'

'*Hulda*, you promised to take care of that. Isn't there a place selling trees right by your office?'

'Yes, there is, I drive past it every day.'

'Then can't you go and buy one first thing tomorrow morning? I suppose we'll be stuck with some spindly little reject now.'

After a moment's silence, Hulda changed the subject. 'Have you got anything else for Dimma? We talked about getting her some jewellery, didn't we? I bought that book

I think she wants – she always used to like reading at Christmas, anyway. And I happen to know that my mother has knitted her a jumper, so at least she'll be safe from the Christmas Cat.' Hulda grinned at her own joke, a reference to the evil cat that, according to folklore, ate Icelandic children who didn't receive any new clothes at Christmas.

'I don't know what she wants,' Jón said. 'She hasn't dropped any hints, but I'll sort it out tomorrow.' Then he added with a chuckle: 'Do you really think she'll wear a jumper knitted by your mum?' Before Hulda could react, he went on: 'This is bloody good wine, isn't it? It certainly cost enough.'

'Yes, it's not bad,' she said, though she wasn't sufficiently used to red wine to be able to taste the difference between plonk and the good stuff. 'Don't make fun of Mum; she's doing her best.' Although she wasn't as close to her mother as she could have wished, Hulda was sometimes hurt by the way Jón talked about her. For her part, Hulda had always been keen for Dimma to get to know her grandmother properly, and that at least had worked out well.

'Your mum hasn't shown her face round here for ages, has she?' Jón remarked, and Hulda knew that the light, teasing note in his voice hid an underlying criticism, though whether of Hulda or her mother, she wasn't sure. Perhaps both of them.

'No, that's my fault. I've just been so busy that I haven't had time to invite her round, to be honest.' It was half true. The fact was, she didn't particularly enjoy her mother's company. Their relationship had always been rather constrained, and her mother could be so suffocatingly intense, always on her back. It's not as if they ever talked about anything that mattered either.

Hulda had spent almost the first two years of her life at a home for infants, and she longed to ask her mother about the past, about why she had been put there. She suspected her grandparents had been mostly to blame, and yet somehow she had found it easier to forgive them than her mother. Naturally, she had been too young to have any memory of her time in the home, but ever since she had learned about it later from her grandfather the knowledge had haunted her. Perhaps that explained her inability to bond with her mother: the feeling that she had been abandoned, that she hadn't been loved, was hard to bear.

She took another sip of Jón's expensive wine. At least she was loved now. Happily married to Jón, mother of a darling daughter. She hoped to goodness Dimma would shake off her sullen mood over Christmas.

Just then she heard a sound from the hall.

'Is she awake?' Hulda asked, starting to get up.

'Sit down, love,' Jón said, placing a hand on her thigh. He was gripping it unnecessarily tightly, she thought, but she didn't protest.

Then she heard a door closing and the click of a lock.

'She's only gone to the bathroom. Calm down, love. We need to give her some space. She's growing up so fast.'

Of course, he was right. Adolescence brought big changes and no doubt children coped with them in different ways. The phase would pass and maybe Hulda simply needed to back off a bit. As a mother, she was tugged by such powerful emotions, but sometimes she knew it would be better if she just relaxed.

They sat in companionable silence for a while, something they'd always been good at. Jón topped up Hulda's glass, though she hadn't emptied it yet, and she thanked him.

'Shouldn't we get a gammon joint to have on the twenty-fourth, as usual?' Jón asked. He obviously hadn't noticed the joint which was already safely stowed in the bottom of the fridge.

'Didn't you two have any supper?' Hulda asked in return. 'And, yes, I've already got the gammon.'

'There was no time. I grabbed a sandwich on my way home and Dimma's used to fending for herself. There's always *skyr* or something in the fridge, isn't there?'

Hulda nodded.

'Busy at work?' he asked amiably, changing the subject.

'Yes, actually. We're always trying to juggle too many cases. There just aren't enough of us.'

'Oh, come on, we live in the most peaceful country in the world.'

She merely smiled, in an attempt to close the subject. Some of the cases she dealt with were deeply distressing and she had no wish to discuss them with him. Then there was the incident that wouldn't stop preying on her mind, although it had happened back in the autumn: the young woman who had vanished in Selfoss. It was a strange business. Perhaps it wouldn't hurt to look at the files again tomorrow.

There was another sound from the hallway. Hulda stood up automatically, ignoring Jón's protest.

She went out into the hall and saw Dimma standing by the door to her room, about to go inside. She paused, her eyes on her mother's, her face as blank as if she were in a world of her own.

'Dimma, darling, are you awake? Is everything all right?' Hulda asked, hearing a note of desperation entering her voice in spite of herself.

She jumped when Jón suddenly put an arm round her shoulders, holding them firmly. Dimma looked at them both in turn, without saying a word, then vanished back into her room.

III

Erla sat facing Einar across the kitchen table. In the background, the voice of the announcer reading the midday news competed with the hiss of static on the old long-wave radio. Reception had always been bad out here and they had been told that they were lucky they could pick up any broadcasts at all. Still, although the quality was up and down, they could usually make out what was being said, even when the interference was at its worst. To Erla, the radio was a lifeline, almost a condition for their continued existence out here. Despite being an avid reader, she couldn't imagine enduring the cold, dark winter months without a radio. Her favourite programmes were plays and serials – anything, really, that would help take her mind off things. She usually served up lunch while listening to the last piece of music before the news, then they would sit down and eat during the midday bulletin, which didn't allow for much conversation. Lunch varied little from day to day: rye bread, sour whey to drink, and heated-up leftovers from the night before, this time in

29

the form of a meat stew. The kitchen was filled with its delicious, hearty smell.

Erla studied her husband. He looked tired. There were shadows under his eyes and deep furrows in his forehead, though he was only in his early fifties. He had worked hard all his life, but there was no end in sight for his labours. They had gradually got out of the habit of seeing old friends and acquaintances from their district and, besides, they were more or less cut off by the state of the roads for several months every year. Einar always used to be fiercely political but now he made do with just buying the party newspaper and casting his vote in every election. He no longer got worked up over current affairs and had given up arguing about politics. Then again, since he and Erla mostly agreed with each other, there was no one for him to argue with, except perhaps the radio.

Despite endless promises, they still couldn't receive television broadcasts. Every year it was a source of friction with those responsible, but, so far, no transmitter covered their area. Then again, maybe it was a good thing not to fall under its spell quite yet. It allowed them to live in the past a little while longer, or so she tried to convince herself. Secretly, though, Erla would have liked a chance to sit down in the evenings in front of the news and those drama series she was always reading about in the papers. There was even a second TV channel these days, but the idea that they would ever be able to receive its broadcasts in this remote valley was nothing but a pipe dream.

'Temperature's dropping, he says,' Einar mumbled after the forecast. Their mealtime conversations far too often revolved around the weather. Of course, it was important, but Erla sometimes missed not being able to move their talk on to a slightly higher plane.

'Mm,' she said, not really listening.

'And yet another damned storm on the way. We're not getting any let-up this winter, just snow, snow and more bloody snow. If it goes on like this, I don't know how our hay stocks are going to last until spring.'

'That's just the way it is, Einar. It's only to be expected. I mean, it's like this every year. We're always trapped here.'

'Well, "trapped" is putting it a bit strongly. Of course it's difficult at the height of winter,' he said, returning his attention to the stew and avoiding Erla's eye.

An unexpected noise made her jump.

It had sounded like someone knocking at the door.

She glanced at her husband. He was sitting frozen into stillness, his spoon halfway to his mouth, his expression astonished. So he had heard it too.

'Anna?' Erla asked. 'Is it Anna?'

Einar didn't answer.

'That was someone knocking at the door, wasn't it, Einar?'

He nodded and got to his feet. Erla copied him and followed as he walked slowly through the sitting room to the hall. Perhaps he thought they'd misheard and it had just been a trick of the wind.

But Erla knew it wasn't.

There was somebody at the door.

IV

Hulda sat in the work canteen, forcing down mouthfuls of skate. She couldn't bear the smell, with its tang of the urinal, and although it didn't taste nearly as bad as you'd expect, it was still far from being her favourite dish. Once a year, on St Thorlákur's Mass, they served up the traditional *kæst skata*, or fermented skate, at the police station, and those who couldn't stand it had to either make do with eating toast amidst the pungent stench, or flee the building and grab something at the local corner shop instead.

That morning she and Jón had asked Dimma if she'd like to go for a burger after they finished work. The suggestion would have been greeted with joy in the old days but this time Dimma had been unenthusiastic. She'd complained of feeling ill and had certainly looked a bit off colour, but when Hulda laid a hand on her forehead there had been no sign of a fever. She hadn't entirely given up hope that the girl would perk up later so they could go out for a special treat after all.

She was also determined to drag Dimma along on a family expedition to Laugavegur later in the evening, to buy a couple more presents and experience the Christmassy atmosphere in the city centre, before returning home to warm up with a hot chocolate. Yes, why not get another little something to put under the tree for Dimma? She could do with cheering up. Maybe Hulda could find a new record for the smart stereo her daughter had been given as a Confirmation gift earlier that year. They could let her open that parcel this evening, after they'd decorated the tree.

One thing was sure, they wouldn't let her get away with sulking like this right through Christmas. Hulda and Jón would have to make a concerted effort to lift their daughter out of her . . . well, her depression. No sooner had Hulda mentally formed the word than she rejected it. A thirteen-year-old could hardly be suffering from depression. On second thoughts, she was ashamed of overreacting like this. It would only make things worse.

Dimma was just a typical moody teenager going through a rebellious phase. *It'll pass*, Hulda reassured herself.

V

There was another bout of knocking, louder than before. Again, Erla flinched.

Einar stood uncertainly by the door for a moment before opening it. Erla hung back at a safe distance behind him.

They were met by a blast of snow as the loose crystals swept in on a gust of wind, then, blinking, made out the shape of a man, well bundled up against the cold, with a thick woollen hat on his head. 'Excuse me, could I come in?' he asked in a low voice.

'Er . . . yes, yes, of course,' Einar said with uncharacteristic hesitation, and Erla could tell from his voice that he was afraid. Einar was hardly ever afraid. But the man didn't appear to be anyone they knew and that in itself was almost unheard of. They never had visitors in winter. In the summers, yes, that was different: they often took in young people who worked in return for meals and accommodation.

'Thank you,' the man said, stepping over the threshold:

'Thank you so much.' He took off his backpack, dislodging a shower of snow, and lowered it to the floor, then sat down on a chair in the hall to remove his boots.

'You're welcome,' Einar replied, sounding a little more confident, Erla thought. 'We don't get many visitors in winter. Well, I say not many, but *none at all* would be more like it. We're not exactly easy to get to.'

The visitor nodded. 'Right.' He had removed one boot and was now fumbling at the laces of the other with numb fingers. The melting snow was dripping off him on to the floor. 'I'm sorry,' he said. 'I should probably have taken my things off outside.'

'Nonsense, come into the warmth, my friend,' Einar said. 'As if we're bothered by a bit of snow in the house. That would be a fine thing!'

'Thanks, I'll mop it up.'

The man took off his other boot, then his coat. His cheeks were flushed with the cold and his eyes looked hollow and red-rimmed with exhaustion.

He'll never be able to get home in time for Christmas, Erla found herself thinking. It wasn't such a bad prospect – from a purely selfish point of view – since they hardly ever had any company during the festive season. According to the forecast on the radio just now, the weather was set to deteriorate, and it would be almost impossible for the man to head back to the village today. Especially as he looked so worn out, though he didn't seem to have any injuries. Her first, automatic reaction had been to check his nose, cheeks and fingers for the telltale signs of frostbite, but they looked fine.

But she grew uneasy. She studied him surreptitiously; there was something about him that made her nervous. Something hard to define. She shrank back instinctively into the sitting room. Einar was still blocking the hall doorway. Although he had invited the man inside, he seemed on edge. After all, there was no getting away from the fact that a complete stranger had entered their home and had, as yet, given no explanation of what he was doing here. No doubt he would account for his presence in a minute.

'We were just finishing lunch,' Einar said. 'Won't you come into the kitchen and have a bite to eat? You must be hungry.'

'Actually, I'd be very grateful,' the man replied. 'To tell the truth, I'm starving.'

'There's bread, and I think there's a bit of stew left over too,' Einar told him.

Erla stayed in the background.

Einar showed the man through the sitting room to the kitchen, with Erla following a few steps behind. The visitor took a good long look around him, as if it was the first time he had ever set foot in an Icelandic farmhouse. And maybe it was.

They sat down at the table. Classical music was playing on the radio, distorted by the usual interference. Their guest fell on his food and for a while no one spoke. Einar and Erla exchanged glances. Should she take the initiative and ask what he was doing there?

'It's nice to have a visitor,' she ventured. 'Makes a pleasant change. I'm Erla, by the way.'

She held out her hand and he shook it.

'And I'm Einar,' added her husband.

'Please excuse my lack of manners,' the man said. 'I was just so tired and hungry. My name's Leó.'

'So, Leó, what brings you out here at this time of year?'

'It's a long story,' he said, and Erla thought she picked up an underlying tension in his voice. 'I was on a trip with two friends from Reykjavík. We were supposed to be home by today but I, well, I managed to lose them.' He gave a rueful sigh.

'You lost them?'

'Well, I think I was the one who got lost. They're both much more experienced than me. I can't imagine how they're feeling right now – they must be worried sick.'

'What were you doing in the area?'

'Shooting ptarmigan. Look, I couldn't possibly borrow your phone, could I? You do have a phone?'

He pushed back his chair and stood up.

'Yes, of course,' Einar replied. 'The line can be a bit crackly in weather like this, but it was all right the last time –'

'Yesterday,' Erla interrupted. 'We made a call yesterday.'

'It's in the sitting room,' Einar went on. 'It can take a few goes to get a connection, as it's a shared line, so you might have to be patient.'

Leó disappeared into the other room.

'I'm not getting a dialling tone,' he called after a while.

Einar stood up and went into the sitting room. 'You don't need to press anything, you should just hear a dialling tone when you pick up the receiver. Though, like

I said, it can take a few tries if other people are using the line.'

Erla stayed where she was in the kitchen, listening as the men tried repeatedly to get a connection.

'Damn it,' Einar said when they came back in. 'The phone's dead. The line must be down.'

'The line? But what . . . what about . . . ?' Erla trailed off. 'Are you sure? It's ages since that last happened.'

'Must be the sheer weight of snow,' Einar said. 'It's a bloody nuisance.'

'Will someone come and sort it out?' Leó asked.

'It depends. Sometimes we have to wait a while for the engineers to fix it. We're not top of their list, as you can imagine.' Einar gave a wry smile. 'I'm afraid this puts you in a difficult position, but I'm damned if I know what to do. The road's impassable for the jeep in these conditions. We don't normally stir from here in the middle of winter.'

'Oh, I see,' said Leó. 'The thing is, I don't know if I feel up to heading back straight away.'

'Goodness, no, of course not. You're welcome to stay here as long as you need to. I was just thinking it must be pretty urgent to get a message to your friends that you're alive.'

'Well, yes, it is. I just hope they don't send out a search party to look for me, but I suppose that's possible.'

'If they do, they're bound to find our place,' Einar said.

'Speaking of which, how did you find us?' Erla chipped in. 'How did you know there were houses up here?'

'What? Is there more than one?'

'There are two, actually,' Einar replied.

'No, I didn't know anyone lived out here at all,' Leó said.

Erla had an uneasy feeling about this visit. She studied the man, who had sat back down at the kitchen table, and tried to work out if he was telling the truth. He was hard to read. His gaze was intent and unwavering but his expression gave little away. She noted that he was strongly built and looked fit. He must be somewhere between forty and fifty. Despite his fatigue, he didn't seem to be in too bad shape for someone who had just been through such an ordeal, but of course appearances could be deceptive.

'I stumbled on this place by pure chance,' he continued. 'An unbelievable stroke of luck. There were markers sticking out of the snow here and there, so I guessed it was a road and tried to follow it. Do you really mean there are only two houses in the entire area?'

'Yes, in a very large area, in fact,' Einar said.

'There are us two on this farm,' Erla elaborated, 'and then our daughter Anna's place, which is a bit of a walk from here.'

'You were extremely lucky,' Einar told him.

'I realize that.' Leó took another mouthful of stew. Erla was sure it must be cold by now, but their guest didn't seem to mind.

'There was nothing about it on the midday news,' she remarked, then immediately wished she hadn't mentioned it.

There was a tense silence. She caught Einar frowning at her, clearly annoyed by her comment.

'About what?' Leó asked after a pause, though it was plain that he knew perfectly well what she meant.

'About you, about the fact you're missing.'

'Oh, well, now you come to mention it, it didn't occur to me that I could end up on the news. My friends are tough guys. I doubt they'd go straight to the police. In fact, I bet they're still trying to track me down themselves. It's not that long since we lost sight of each other and they've got a map of the area, or at least one of them has. Your farm's definitely marked on the map, isn't it? I expect they're on their way here as we speak.' He smiled awkwardly.

'On some maps, yes. Still, I imagine they'll turn up soon if you got separated on the moors near here. It would make sense.'

The conversation petered out and no one said anything for a while. Erla didn't like to stare at their visitor while he was eating, so she swung her gaze back and forth between her husband and the window. It wasn't snowing, but a fierce wind was blowing outside and the whole house chimed in as usual, while icy draughts sought out every chink in the walls or window frames. When the temperature plummeted, like it had yesterday evening, the heating was powerless against the cold. Today was a little milder, though presumably still below freezing. But then it was highly unusual for the mercury to rise above zero in midwinter.

'Thanks very much,' Leó said at last, his bowl empty. He had polished off most of the bread too.

'You'll stay with us – we have a spare room for guests down the passage,' Einar said.

'That's very kind, thank you.'

'I would offer to guide you back to the village tomorrow, but it's Christmas Eve, you see, so it's a bit difficult for me to be away from home. And it's quite a long trek – I'm sure you understand. But you're welcome to stay with us over Christmas. I can accompany you back afterwards, or just put you on the right track, if you'd prefer.'

'The last thing I want to do is upset your Christmas plans,' Leó hastened to assure them. 'I'll try and head off tomorrow morning, assuming I've recovered by then. I expect I'll crash out good and early this evening after today's little adventure.' He broke off to yawn. 'And then I'll get going first thing and leave you to enjoy your Christmas in peace.'

Erla was still feeling inexplicably twitchy in their visitor's presence; there was something about his manner that bothered her, that didn't ring true. Something vaguely threatening. That unnervingly intent stare. 'Your family must be wondering where you are,' she said. It was a statement rather than a question.

Leó's reaction was odd. His face twisted in a grimace and he didn't immediately reply, then after a pause he answered, as if he couldn't bear the silence any longer: 'No, there's nobody waiting for me.'

'It's an unusual time of year for a shooting trip,' Erla persisted. She was having a hard time believing a word he said and was only surprised that Einar was being so forbearing. Perhaps it was just his innate good manners. As a true countryman, her husband had been brought up never to refuse anyone hospitality. 'So close to Christmas, I mean.'

Again, there was a delay before Leó answered: 'Me and my friends aren't that big on Christmas, to be honest – though we were planning to drive back to town tomorrow morning. Not that we'll be able to now, which is a bit of a bugger.' He smiled. 'Excuse my language. I can't tell you how happy I was to see your lights. I was totally lost and scared to death that . . . well, that I'd be caught out by nightfall.'

'Oh, the nights here are something else,' Erla said quietly, but with such feeling that Leó looked a little taken aback. 'I hope you're not afraid of the dark.'

'God, no, I'm sure I'll be fine. Anyway, what do, er, how do you pass the time in the long winter evenings? I don't suppose you can get TV up here?'

'No, thank God!' Einar said with feeling. Erla shot him a glance, aware that he was eager to change the subject and prevent her from continuing what amounted almost to an interrogation of the man.

'Then perhaps we can sit down this evening and have a proper talk,' said Leó, with an odd inflection to his voice.

'Erla, why don't you show Leó to the spare room?' Einar asked.

She stood up reluctantly. She would rather Leó left right now. Realizing that she was nervous about sleeping under the same roof as him, she told herself off for being silly. What possible reason could he have for wanting to harm them? And, anyway, they were two against one.

'Thanks.' He smiled warmly, looking her straight in the eye, and for a moment she felt ashamed of her suspicions.

He was a good-looking man, tall, with thick black hair shot through with grey. 'Thank you so much again. I don't know what would have happened to me if I hadn't found you.'

Again, she remembered that there had been nothing about a missing man on the news. It was worrying, but of course there could be a perfectly natural explanation.

'I've just got to go and check on the animals,' Einar said. 'Make yourself at home, Leó, and feel free to stay with us as long as you like.'

Erla led the way to the spare room, which was next door to Anna's old bedroom. It wasn't very big and they rarely used it, so it smelled a bit stale. She opened the window, admitting an icy draught that sent the curtains flapping wildly. The furniture consisted of a shabby old divan, a chest of drawers and a bedside table. The chest was used for bedlinen and old clothes of theirs and Anna's that they no longer wore. On top were a number of framed photographs, some of Einar's parents and various relations, others from their own collection, including a black-and-white snapshot from back when Erla and Einar had first met, when they were young and foolish and used to spend their free time bumping over the country's rough gravel roads in an old wreck of a car. Even then it had been on the cards that Einar would have to take over the farm, but at the time she hadn't fully grasped what that would mean. Subconsciously, she had hoped they'd eventually be able to make a life for themselves in the capital instead, even go on the odd foreign holiday, but none of these dreams had come true.

Then there was the family portrait of them with Anna as a beautiful, red-haired teenager.

'There are sheets in there,' she said, pointing to the chest and trying not to sound too offhand.

'Thanks, thank you.' He was staring at her so intently that she began to feel uncomfortable again. It was as if he were trying to figure her out. But perhaps, as so often, she was simply letting her imagination run away with her.

He took a step or two towards her and she recoiled, believing for an instant that he was going to attack her. But to her relief, he stopped and said politely: 'I think I'll have a bit of a lie-down. I'm feeling pretty shattered.'

Erla nodded and slipped past him, out of the room.

'I'm going to join Einar in the barn. Come and find us if you need anything,' she said. 'With any luck, you'll be home tomorrow,' she added as a parting shot, and closed the door firmly behind her.

She wasn't in the habit of helping Einar with the feeding, since he was perfectly capable of managing on his own, but she didn't want to be alone in the house with that stranger. She pulled on a thick woollen *lopapeysa*, a padded down jacket and boots, then went out into the cold. In fact, the cold wasn't the worst part. She enjoyed filling her lungs with the clean air blown in with the winter winds and her warm clothes kept out the worst of the frost. The scene that met her eyes was bleak and featureless, all landmarks obliterated by a smothering whiteness. It was a grey day, the clouds swollen with unshed snow, scudding overhead with the fierce wind, and in another couple of hours it would be dark. It was the darkness that got to her. In winter, when the nights closed in, she avoided going outside at all if she could help it, so she didn't have to witness the unrelieved gloom stretching out as far as the eye could see, without the faintest pinprick of light anywhere to give one hope. Anna's house was too far off, hidden by higher ground, for the glow from her windows to be visible. Only when the moon was shining could Erla bear to go out in the evenings. The moon was her friend; they got on well together. But even in the moonlight there was no getting away from the isolation, the cursed isolation. The crushing knowledge that she couldn't go anywhere; that if anything went wrong, it might not be possible to get help . . . She hastily pushed these thoughts away.

Although there was a temporary let-up in the snow, judging by the threatening sky it wouldn't be long before it started coming down heavily again. The drifts mounted up at this time of year and froze hard in the bitter temperatures, lasting until February if they were lucky; into March if they were not.

It was then that she spotted Leó's footprints. Without really knowing why, she started to follow them down the slope, noting that he had indeed followed the road, as he had said. The only road. The road that led here from the village, first to Anna's, then to their farm.

The guest had clearly indicated that he hadn't seen another house. How was that possible, unless he had been lying? In spite of the cold, she broke out in a sweat under her thick woollen jumper and coat. Slowly, deliberately, she turned, hearing only the moaning of the wind, blinkered by her hood. She was suddenly convinced that their visitor, Leó – if that was really his name – had followed her outside and was standing right behind her.

There was nobody there. She was standing alone in the snow, allowing herself to be frightened by imaginary phantoms, as so often before.

She began wading back towards the farmhouse as fast as she could go, her boots sinking in the powdery drifts, slowing her down until she felt as if she were caught in a bad dream, struggling, unable to make any headway.

Reaching the front door at last, she opened it and stamped on the mat to remove the worst of the snow, then glanced up quickly, because now she really had seen a ghost. Her heart lurched as she found herself looking straight into Leó's white face. He was standing in the passage, but she could have sworn that he had just emerged, hastily, from her and Einar's bedroom.

VI

'All we can think of is that she must have accepted a lift with the wrong man,' said the police inspector over the phone from Selfoss. 'Nothing else has turned up at our end that can shed any light on the case.'

'I see,' said Hulda. It bothered her that the incident remained unsolved, although there was every chance the girl's disappearance had been deliberate. Sadly, suicide wasn't that uncommon. But another theory the police had considered at the time was that she might have hitched a lift with a driver who had attacked her.

The girl, a twenty-year-old from the upmarket Reykjavík suburb of Garðabær, had been taking a year off between school and university. She came from a good family: her father was a lawyer, her mother a nurse. Hulda had spoken to the parents repeatedly in the course of the investigation but hadn't detected any hint of problems at home. All the indications were that she was a perfectly normal girl who had simply vanished into thin air.

'What about at your end?' asked the inspector from Selfoss.

'Our end?'

'How's the inquiry going? You're in charge of it, aren't you?'

'Oh, yes, I am,' said Hulda. 'We're making zero progress, I'm afraid. The trail's gone completely cold. That's why I'm calling. I was hoping something new might have turned up.'

When last heard of, the girl had been staying in an old summer house outside the small town of Selfoss, in the southern lowlands some fifty kilometres east of Reykjavík. Her parents had heard from her while she was there, and the locals had been aware of her presence, but after that nothing more was known of her movements. The police had examined every inch of the summer house but could find no evidence of a struggle or any signs that anyone else had been there. The girl's belongings had vanished too, which suggested that she had left of her own volition.

The police had combed the banks of the Ölfúsá, the milky glacial river that flowed through the town, as well as a wide swathe of the countryside around the summer house. They had searched the neighbouring buildings and put out an appeal for information, but no one had come forward. At this point, the worrying suspicion had occurred to the police that she might, as the inspector put it, have got into a car with the wrong man. She was young, vulnerable and stunningly pretty, judging from the photos of the tall, willowy redhead. And quite an experienced traveller too, in spite of her youth. Everyone agreed that she had been a lovely girl, and a budding artist as well – she had taken time off to concentrate on her writing and painting. 'She was very artistic,' her mother had said during one of Hulda's visits to the parents' affluent, middle-class home: 'Her poems had such a pure, heartfelt simplicity. And she was finally pursuing her dream of writing a novel too.'

The case had been all over the news, as such disappearances were unusual in Iceland's small, peaceful island community and very rarely the result of murder. But, as time passed, Hulda got the impression that most people had come to the conclusion that the girl must have taken her own life, although the police had no particular reason to believe this.

'I'll let you know if there are any developments, Hulda,' the inspector went on, 'but I wouldn't get your hopes up. It must have been some pervert, you know; some sick bastard who conned her into accepting a lift with him and . . . and, well, assaulted her. We've seen that sort of thing before. And it always ends badly. I'm convinced she's dead, convinced of it. The evidence will turn up sooner or later, but I don't think there's anything we can do in the meantime.'

Although Hulda agreed with this, she felt a sense of duty towards the girl. It was her case and she had failed to solve it. And, quite apart from that, she needed something to take her mind off her own problems. Dimma's constant moodiness was making life increasingly difficult at home.

'Isn't there anything we can do?' she asked. 'Any leads I could follow up, however minor?'

There was silence at the other end, then her colleague said: 'Just go home to your family, Hulda. It's almost Christmas, after all.'

Hulda said a curt goodbye and put down the receiver, seething slightly.

Things were quiet at work; everyone was looking forward to Christmas and there were no major investigations underway, nothing urgent that couldn't wait until after the holidays. Since Hulda had to take the shift on 25 December, she could have left a bit early today, popped into town and bought some jewellery for her daughter on the way home, as she had planned. But she knew she wouldn't do it. She had a constant battle to prove herself in the patriarchal world of the police and couldn't afford to show any sign of weakness. She didn't want to be 'the mother' who left work early on St Thorlákur's Mass, prioritizing her family over her job. She had to be seen to be more dedicated than her male counterparts. It was just a fact of life.

She went back to leafing through the files, but her thoughts were all of Dimma.

VII

Unnur went back into the summer house one last time to make sure she hadn't forgotten anything. Her stay there had been exceptionally pleasant and peaceful. That summer she had mostly let herself be guided by chance, temporarily free from the fetters of education; freer than ever before. The decision to take a year off had surprised her more than anyone, but it had turned out to be easier than she had anticipated. She had always been among the top in her class at school, and her parents, that conventional Gardabær couple, had naturally assumed she would go straight to university. To be honest, she had always pictured herself following that path as well, but then a friend of hers had said she was going abroad for a year to 'find herself'. Unnur had no need to find herself, as she wasn't lost, but the idea struck her as a good one. To spend a year doing whatever she liked, meeting new people, and maybe writing a bit too. Perhaps that was the real reason, when she thought about it: she wanted to write a book. She'd been constantly scribbling ever since she was a child, and for the last few years she'd been walking around with the germ of an idea for a novel. She had considered going abroad, like her friend, but in the end she had decided to travel around Iceland instead. *Leave the whole thing up to fate.* She didn't know where she was going and didn't have a lot of money, so she would have to be resourceful. Of course, she could have asked her parents for a loan, but she didn't want to; for the first time in her life she wanted to stand on her own two feet.

She had spent the last few weeks staying in this old summer house, just outside Selfoss. True to her plan, it had been by pure coincidence that she had ended up here, as she had heard via her friend of a house that was lent out to artists. Unnur had got in touch with the owner on the off chance, well aware that she didn't really qualify as an artist yet, despite her ambition to write a book. The woman who owned it had turned out to be a pensioner. They had drunk coffee together and hit it off immediately. The upshot was that the woman had agreed to lend Unnur the house, 'for as long as you need it, dear. Just leave the key under the mat when you go.' And now Unnur felt it was time to move on. The novel was going fairly well; she'd filled one exercise book and was part of the way through a second. She had met nice people too. Although the nearest neighbours lived some way off, Unnur had gone out of her way to be sociable by making frequent trips into Selfoss. It was essential to mix with all types if she was going to be a writer. Unlike her friend, she hadn't undertaken this journey as a voyage of self-discovery but to learn about other people's lives, to gain experience and improve her understanding of the world. Then, hopefully, she would be able to get all the thoughts that were whirling around in her head down on paper and turn them into a book.

Having reassured herself that she hadn't left anything behind in the summer house, she locked the door and put the key conscientiously under the mat. All her possessions, the most precious of which were her exercise books, fitted into one large backpack. What she needed now was to move on to somewhere new and meet new people in a different environment. It didn't really matter where, and she hadn't made any specific plans. To be free as a bird – the thought made her heart sing.

Unnur walked unhurriedly along the road towards Selfoss. There was little traffic at this early hour. She was used to having to get up at the crack of dawn for school and that hadn't changed just because she was her own mistress these days, with no obligations. The way she saw it, self-discipline was essential if you wanted to become a successful novelist. And she found the lifestyle suited her so well that she had even begun to wonder if she should forget her plans to go to university. Of course, she knew this idea was bound to meet with opposition from her parents, and perhaps it was an illusion, a vision of the future that appealed to her now but that wouldn't survive the cold light of day once she returned to her old life. Still, whatever happened, she was determined to finish her book.

She knew from experience that it could take a while to get a lift. Very few drivers were prepared to stop and pick up a stranger. When they did stop, they almost without exception addressed her in English, although they were clearly Icelanders, since they couldn't believe that anyone except a foreign tourist would stand on the side of the road, hitching a lift. It pleased her to think that she didn't fit any of the usual stereotypes. Her mother would never have dreamt of letting her hitchhike round the country, so she had lied to her and said she was planning to rely on buses. Apart from that, she had told her parents as little as possible, merely that she meant to spend a whole year travelling in Iceland, meeting new people and taking jobs here and there to support herself. From time to time she sent them letters, and in return they left her completely to her own devices. They trusted her. All she had promised was that, once the

*year was up, she would come home to Gardabær and enrol at the
university.*

*Several cars had passed while she had been walking, but no one
had paid her any attention. That was all right; she was in no hurry.
The next stage of her adventure was just beginning. She was hoping
to be able to work in exchange for a roof over her head but could
afford to pay for accommodation if necessary. She had brought along
her savings and, while she wasn't exactly loaded, she knew how to
make her money last. There was the knowledge, too, that her parents would send her anything she asked for, which was a useful safety
net, though she had no intention of using it. Not unless she was
desperate . . . It irritated Unnur a little that she had grown up in
such a privileged home. She wanted to be independent, to prove that
she could look after herself, and only now, finally, did she feel the
umbilical cord had been truly cut.*

*Hearing the sound of an approaching engine, she paused at the
side of the road and turned round. It was an old white BMW. Her
parents used to have a car like that. Unnur stuck out her thumb
and the driver slowed down. At last. Now she could take the next
step, though her destination remained tantalizingly unknown.*

VIII

Erla stood on the mat as if turned to stone, unable to utter a word. Her heart began to pound and she was, for the first time in ages, genuinely frightened.

'I was just looking for, you know, the toilet,' said Leó. He was lying, she was sure of it. The bedroom door had stood open, as always, and there was no way he could have confused it with the toilet. The bathroom door had been open too, right next to the spare room, so he could hardly have failed to notice it.

'It's . . .' she stammered, '. . . it's down there, next to your room.'

'Oh, yes, of course, of course, I remember now.' He smiled. It was a charming smile in its way, but Erla found it oddly menacing. She rapidly changed her mind about asking Leó any difficult questions without Einar there as back-up. Her anger had been quickly replaced by fear. Ignoring the impulse to go into their bedroom and check that he hadn't touched anything, she decided to go straight back outside, however strange it might look, and find Einar.

She watched her husband feeding the sheep, her heart still beating unnaturally fast. The air in the barn was full of the familiar sounds of bleating and munching, the sweet scent of hay mingling with the odours of dung and wool, and the warmth rising from the milling backs of the ewes. She used to take pleasure in the company of the animals, but over the years she had grown to resent them as yet another link in the chain that held her prisoner here.

She wondered if she should say anything or just remain alert and keep an eye on their visitor while staying close to Einar. Simply trust that nothing bad would happen and that Leó would leave in the morning. Yet she had a horrible premonition that this was wishful thinking on her part.

'Are you all right, love?' Einar asked. Her anxiety must show in her face.

'Yes, fine. I'm just a bit uneasy about that man. I don't like having him here.'

'Uneasy? Why? We're used to having visitors from time to time, love.'

'I know, but that's different.'

'Different in what way? We always get the odd paying guest in summer as well as the usual helpers. They're strangers too. You've even had guests here when you were on your own.'

'I know.'

'The only difference is that we're not going to charge the poor bloke anything. It wouldn't be fair. It's our duty to offer him shelter. Don't you agree? Or did you want to ask him to pay?'

'Pay? No, of course not, that's not what I meant at all, Einar. Are you saying you don't find the whole thing a bit odd?'

'We're just not used to seeing people out here in winter, love. But that doesn't mean it can't happen. Please, let's not be like this. Let's just show the poor man some hospitality. He'll soon be on his way.'

She nodded, resigned.

IX

Darkness had fallen outside. Einar and Erla were sitting at the supper table with their guest. The news was on in the background, the announcer's voice crackling and distorted with static, carrying over mountain, moor and cold volcanic desert, all the way from the capital on the other side of the country. Erla saw the kitchen for a moment through their guest's eyes. The yellow and white units, inherited from Einar's parents, were not what they would have chosen for themselves. The heavy wooden table was an heirloom too, but Erla had bought the chairs herself. At first it had been a constant source of irritation to have to live in someone else's home, surrounded by their taste, their furnishings, but she had grown used to it over the years. She really couldn't care less any more.

So far, she had contributed nothing to the conversation, leaving Einar to do the talking.

'Don't people eat skate here?' Leó asked, tucking into the roast lamb Erla had served up.

'It's not something we've ever done,' Einar told him.

'It was never the custom here in the east when I was a boy. Which is fine by me, as I have absolutely no desire to eat rotten fish!' Laughter rumbled in his chest.

'How's the farming going?'

'Don't get me started! It's a constant hard slog, but we struggle on. If I go, there won't be a single farm left in the whole valley, and I don't want that on my gravestone.'

'Isn't it inevitable, though? I mean, times are changing.'

'Well, I'm old-fashioned enough to think that people should keep working the land. But I see you're new to all this. I don't suppose you've ever spent any time on a farm before.'

'No, you're right, I haven't,' Leó said. 'But I admire your tenacity.'

Erla was sitting bolt upright, staring at Leó. She'd hardly touched her dinner. He seemed aware of her tension, flicking the odd glance at her while keeping up a friendly flow of conversation with Einar. She was fighting back the urge to interrupt their small talk to ask Leó just what the hell he was up to. Why had he come there and what did he want from them? But perhaps she ought to try and discuss it with Einar again first.

'How often do you manage to leave the farm in winter?' Leó asked.

'Not often. The road's more or less closed in the coldest months,' Einar explained, 'or difficult to drive on, anyway. We're not well connected enough for them to bother sending the snow ploughs out this far, you see. And someone has to be here to feed the sheep.'

'Nobody cares about us,' Erla chipped in.

'I wouldn't go that far.' Einar smiled awkwardly. 'Though I'm sure if we were – oh, I don't know – on the local council or in with our MP, there might be more pressure to keep the road open for longer. It's all about politics – all about who you know. But then I expect it's the same in Reykjavík too?'

Leó didn't immediately answer, then said: 'Yes, now you come to mention it, I suppose it is.'

Watching him, Erla got the impression that Leó was someone who had never had to worry about not knowing the right people. He looked as if he led a comfortable life, with no shortage of money. His clothes were obviously expensive and showed no signs of wear, making her acutely aware of how shabby she and Einar appeared in comparison. And his hesitation in answering had seemed genuine, as if he had never actually given any thought to how people might struggle without the right connections.

It wasn't exactly common for city types to go on shooting trips in the mountains at this time of year. No, it was a rich man's sport. If only she and Einar had that kind of money . . . Then maybe they could live somewhere else and get tenants to take care of the farm. Erla knew Einar would never agree to sell the land, but she sometimes fantasized about moving without selling up, seeing this as a compromise that he might just be prepared to accept. With this aim in mind, she bought a lottery ticket whenever she went into the village. The girl in the shop always smiled when she came in: 'Lottery time again, Erla?' she'd say, then add some comment like: 'You know, I've got a feeling this could be your lucky day.' Her dream wasn't that far-fetched. A ticket with five winning numbers had been sold in a shop in the neighbouring village not so long ago. Needless to say, the winner had moved to Reykjavík.

'Help yourself to —' Einar broke off in the middle of what he was saying as the kitchen lights started to flicker.

'What's happening?' Leó asked.

It looked as if the electricity was about to go. The lights kept dimming alarmingly, then brightening again as if nothing had happened.

'It's nothing new,' Einar said. 'Power cuts are part of our daily life out here. Well, not daily, obviously, but they're far too common.'

'Damn, I didn't expect that.'

'Welcome to the countryside, mate. We're used to it. We always have candles at the ready and carry matches in our pockets. We use torches too, of course, but I find candles cosier.' Einar took a box of matches out of his breast pocket and shook it as if for emphasis. 'Always prepared.' His smile looked a little constrained and Erla sensed that he was troubled. Was it beginning to dawn on him that there was something odd about Leó's visit? Perhaps the threat of a power cut, on top of the strange coincidence of the phone stopping working, had got him worried.

'They still haven't reported you missing,' Erla murmured, just loud enough for both men to hear.

'I wasn't listening, actually,' Leó said. It was a feeble excuse. They wouldn't have failed to notice if there had been mention of a lost ptarmigan hunter on the radio. 'And the news isn't over yet.'

Neither Einar nor Erla said anything. Leó dropped his eyes to his plate and took a mouthful of lamb. The news-reader droned away in the background. 'I expect they're all still searching for me and haven't come down from the mountain yet. I . . . I'm sure that's why. They'd do a thorough search of the area themselves before going to get help.'

'All?' Erla queried, pouncing on the word. 'How many of them are there, then?'

'Mm?' Leó sounded puzzled. 'Three.'

'Oh, that's strange,' Erla said, careful to remain out-wardly composed. She hoped he couldn't hear from her voice how fast her heart was beating or how troubled she was underneath.

'Strange?' It was Einar who asked. 'Why?'

Erla looked at her husband, then back at their visitor: 'I thought you said earlier that you'd been out shooting with *two* friends? That there were only three of you in total?'

Although visibly disconcerted, Leó was quick to retort: 'Did I say that? Two? No, there are three of them. There were four of us altogether. You . . . you don't go on a trip like that in winter without, without . . . plenty of back-up.' It was blatantly obvious to Erla that he was lying.

He returned her gaze with a challenging stare and she could have sworn that for an unguarded moment there was a flash of pure hostility in his eyes, before he quickly mastered it and resumed his bland expression.

The lights flickered again and Erla shivered.

Einar seized the excuse to change the subject. 'Bloody power cuts.' This was typical of him. Apart from good-humoured wrangling about politics, he had never been able to stand conflict of any kind, whether verbal or physical, and always went out of his way to avoid confrontation. Like water, he was adept at finding the path of least resistance. Until he was pushed too far, that is. Then she never knew how he'd react. But that's just the way her Einar was and there was no changing him. You couldn't teach an old dog new tricks, and all that. No, Erla knew it was up to her to take the initiative, as usual. Up to her to get rid of this potentially dangerous man.

'Bloody power cuts,' Einar repeated. 'The electricity often goes at Christmas, I'm afraid.'

'At Christmas? That must be a pain.'

'Yes, it is, but it can't be helped,' Einar said. 'Christmas puts such a strain on the system, you see. But we're used to making the best of things. Aren't we, love?'

Erla nodded, without a word.

'We just open our presents and read by candlelight. It's grand, actually. Reminds me of the old days. My family's lived here for centuries, you know. It's our ancestral stamping ground. Our little patch of earth. And you have to look after your own.'

'You can say that again.'

'What do you do yourself, Leó?' Erla asked. 'You said you were here with friends from Reykjavík. I take it you live there?'

'What? Oh, yes, I live in Reykjavík. That's right. I'm a teacher.'

'School's broken up, then?'

'That's right.'

'Which school is that?'

'Which school?' he repeated, as if to win time.

Hasn't he rehearsed his story better than that? Erla thought to herself.

'The university, actually,' he said. 'I teach at the university.'

'What?' Erla asked, then clarified: 'What do you teach?'

'Psychology.'

'Well I never, you're a psychologist, are you? I hope you're not planning to analyse us!' Einar said with mock alarm, but the joke failed to dispel the tension.

'No risk of that.' Leó's smile was forced.

The lights dimmed again.

'You know, I'm afraid we really are in for a power cut. It always starts like this. Have you got a candle in your room for the night, Leó?' Einar looked first at their guest, then inquiringly at Erla.

'I don't think there's a candle in his room,' she answered after a pause. 'But I'm sure we can find a spare one, since it's only for the one night. After all, he's leaving tomorrow morning. I assume you'll be setting off early, Leó? As soon as it gets light?'

'Yes, absolutely. That's the plan.'

'Take the matches.' Einar handed him the box from his breast pocket. 'We've got another box in our room. And don't let the darkness get to you, mate.'

'Thanks for supper. It was very good.'

'Erla's an excellent cook. Are you sure you wouldn't like any more?'

'Thanks, but I couldn't, I'm stuffed. You're real life-savers. I'm feeling a lot better already. You should open a guesthouse.' He looked at them both in turn.

Einar smiled. 'We do get visitors from time to time, so we're used to it. Only last summer, well, late summer, there were a couple of lads from Reykjavík – nice kids. Stayed with us for three or four days. Which reminds me, Erla, I posted their letter last time I went to the village.'

'Their letter?'

'Yes, I found a letter that must have slipped down between the books in the guestroom, so I took it with me. I expect they'll have been wondering what happened to it – or rather the person it was addressed to will.'

'That must . . .' Leó paused as if searching for the right words, then went on: 'Everything clearly moves at its own pace here in the countryside.'

'You can say that again,' Einar replied. 'The papers are always out of date by the time they reach us, and the clock stopped years ago!' His laughter had a hollow ring.

Erla's gaze was drawn to the window. It had started to snow again, quietly, inexorably covering Leó's tracks, obliterating the evidence of his lie. But she knew and that was enough. She would have to be on her guard and take care for both of them. However pretty the white flakes looked as they danced past the window, to her they were ominous. She could feel the snow piling up, surrounding her, hemming her in. It would be a white Christmas, as usual. Stiflingly white. And now this intruder had entered their peaceful home and poisoned the atmosphere. You couldn't describe it any other way. He'd poisoned it. The wind whined outside – hardly a harbinger of peace on earth and goodwill to all men.

'Shall we move into the sitting room?' Einar stood up. 'And how about some coffee?'

'Sounds great,' said Leó, following Einar's example.

'I'll put some on.' Erla watched the men go through to the other room.

She fetched the packet of coffee from the cupboard, counted out the measures for three cups, filled the machine with water and switched it on, hoping the electricity wouldn't go before it had finished. As she watched the drops percolating into the jug, one after the other, she listened to the murmur of the men's voices from the sitting room. The radio was still on; it was the weather forecast now. She turned it off. She didn't need it to tell her that they were in for another snowstorm.

Erla took the coffee through and poured a cup for herself as well. She meant to drink plenty so the caffeine would keep her awake and alert tonight. 'Milk or sugar?' she asked Leó. She had no need to ask her husband: heavy on the milk, heavy on the sugar.

'Just black, thanks.'

She sat down, and for a while no one said anything. The curtains were open and, outside, they could see the snow falling, or rather being whirled past the window.

'That's a fine Christmas tree you've got there,' their visitor said at last, as if to fill the silence.

Erla chose not to answer. Rudeness didn't come naturally to her, but she had no intention of playing along with this man, chatting away as if nothing was the matter. All she could think about was getting rid of him as soon as possible. It had to be made abundantly clear to him that he was unwelcome here. Even though she wasn't always that happy in this house, it was her and Einar's home, her sanctuary. But now she felt as if both her peace of mind and her safety were under threat.

'Yes, though it's rather a whopper this time,' Einar replied. 'It wasn't meant to be that big, but it's hard to picture how large it is until you get the tree into the sitting room.'

'Well, I must say, it all looks nice and festive. Have you lived here long?'

Far too long, Erla wanted to say, but bit her lip.

'All my life,' Einar said, his pride audible. 'Erla's from Reykjavík, but she took on the farm when she agreed to take on me. It's a good place to live. You know, you get used to the silence and the fact nothing ever happens out here. Of course, it's not for everyone, but I reckon Erla's adapted pretty well. It must be quite a change for you, though?'

'You can say that again. I was brought up with the constant noise and bustle of the city. I'm almost sorry to have to hurry off in the morning, as it must be very special experiencing Christmas here, in the snow and the solitude.'

'Yes, well, you'll miss all that,' Erla said pointedly.

'It's always quiet here, of course,' Einar went on, trying

to smooth over her rudeness. 'Nothing ever happens. But we make an occasion of it. Have a special meal, treat ourselves, you know. And we listen to the Christmas service when the long-wave reception is clear enough, though it's a bit touch and go, as you can imagine after hearing the news earlier. Sometimes it's just as well to know most of the hymns off by heart, so it doesn't matter if you can't hear the words.' He chuckled.

'I suppose it's quite a trek to the nearest church,' Leó said.

'You're right about that. There's absolutely no point us trying to make it to church in winter. I remember how that used to upset my mother in the old days, but Erla and I have tried not to let it bother us. You can get used to most things eventually.'

'And . . .' Leó turned to Erla: 'What about your daughter? Will she be coming round tomorrow? You mentioned she lived nearby?'

'Of course she's coming,' Erla said at once, sharply. 'She'll be here in the morning. Though I don't suppose you'll meet her because you'll be gone by then, Leó.'

'How . . . how old is she?' Leó asked after an embarrassed pause.

Erla didn't answer immediately as she was thinking hard about what to say. It was time to expose the man's lies. She shot a glance at Einar, trying to convey the message: *I'll take care of this.*

'You should know,' she said then, in a harsh, almost accusatory tone.

The words had quite an impact on Leó. He jerked back

on the sofa, where he was sitting, and spilt some coffee on himself.

'I'm sorry?' he said, with a quick intake of breath.

The lights flickered again, more alarmingly this time, the darkness lasting longer before they came back on. The brief blackout distracted them from the conversation, giving the visitor an excuse to dodge her question, and he took full advantage of it: 'God, I'm not used to this. Is there nothing we can do to sort it out – to stop the power going completely, I mean? You haven't got a generator, have you?'

'Not a single thing, I'm afraid,' Einar said with a grin. 'We've never got round to installing a generator. They're just too expensive.'

Erla had the feeling he was getting a secret kick out of teasing the city boy. She watched Leó sitting there sipping his coffee. It would have been so easy to slip a couple of her sleeping pills into his cup, so she could rest easier tonight. She regretted not having thought of it before . . . As it was, she doubted she would shut her eyes at all.

'Thanks for the coffee,' Leó said, although he hadn't finished it, 'and for the hospitality. I'm very grateful to you both.'

'No need to rush off to bed,' said Einar. 'Erla and I are enjoying having some company for a change.'

'It's kind of you to say so, but I'm fading a bit, to be honest. And it *is* St Thorlákur's Mass, after all. I expect you had other plans.' He smiled. 'Doing the last-minute Christmas preparations and all that.'

No plans at all, Erla thought to herself. She had long ago got everything ready, with no help from Einar, who, despite what he said, was fairly indifferent to the occasion. Most days were alike to him and he could hardly be bothered to vary his routine for Christmas, Easter, or any other high days or holidays, for that matter. They never went anywhere and it was always left to Erla to make an effort. There were times when she'd considered doing nothing at all for Christmas and waiting to see if he even noticed. If he'd say anything if she didn't ask him to cut down a fir tree; if she just served up blood sausage on the twenty-fourth and didn't give him any presents.

'Do stay up a bit longer,' Einar said. 'At least finish your coffee.'

'Thanks, I will,' Leó replied, though he looked as if he'd rather be elsewhere. His gaze wandered round the room. Erla wasn't sure if he was looking for something in particular or just trying to work out an escape route from this oppressive threesome.

'How big's this house?' he asked abruptly, as if in a rather desperate attempt to hit on a subject to talk about.

'Big? How many square metres, you mean?' Einar asked. 'Oh, I can't remember. It's not something I've had to think about recently. After all, it's not as if I'm planning to sell. We mean to grow old here, Erla and I.' He threw her a smile, but she didn't return it.

'All on the one floor, I suppose?'

'Yes, that's right, though we do have a small attic.'

'Oh, right, a loft for storage, you mean?'

'Yes, box rooms, and a little room where we put up the

youngsters who come to help out on the farm, and the odd paying guest as well.'

'In that case, why don't you put me up there? I'd be less in your way.'

'No, no, out of the question. There's no radiator up there. You'll be much more comfortable where you are now. We usually keep it private and put visitors upstairs, but you've been through a rough time and we're not going to stick you upstairs in the cold. We don't want to risk you catching a chill. It's our duty to look after people who get caught out in storms or lost on the moors. You could have died of exposure, you do realize that? Going out like that with no proper equipment and unused to conditions in the highlands . . . I'm sure your friends realize they're to blame. They should have known better and made sure everyone in the group was equipped with a compass, a map, and so on. It was extremely reckless of them.' Einar's voice had thickened with disapproval.

Leó shook his head and said charitably: 'I wouldn't want to blame them, they're good guys. It's my fault, really. I should have taken more care. After all, I'm responsible for myself. Ultimately, we're all responsible for ourselves, aren't we?'

'I certainly believe that,' Einar said, but Erla remained tight-lipped.

'Well, anyway, you've got a charming home, very snug,' Leó went on.

'Yes, we're happy here,' Einar said.

'I assume you've got a cellar as well?'

'A cellar? Oh, right, yes, a cellar. Anyone would think

you wanted to buy the place!' Einar laughed so hard at his own joke that he almost spilt coffee on his checked shirt.

'Oh, ha, ha, no, it's a bit too remote for me. No, I'm just interested. Just making conversation.'

'There's nothing of interest down there, just a freezer and food supplies, and so on,' Erla said in a low voice, glaring at their uninvited guest.

'Er, OK. I wasn't actually planning to go down there,' Leó replied, trying to make a joke of it.

He looked at her searchingly, but she averted her gaze, shifting it to the window instead, where she could see the sitting room mirrored in the glass.

'Did you stop by at Anna's house on your way here?' she asked, apropos of nothing, watching his reflection in the window.

'Erla, please –' Einar began, but she cut across him, determined to get to the bottom of this.

'Did you stop by her place?' she asked again.

'Sorry, I don't understand the question.'

'Anna, our daughter. I told you she lives in the next house, twenty minutes or so down the road. You passed it on your way here, didn't you?' As she said it, she felt a sudden, sickening fear that something might have happened to her daughter, that this stranger might have hurt her somehow . . .

'No, I've, er, already told you. I came straight here. I didn't pass any other houses on the way.'

Erla was now convinced that Leó was lying to them about who he was and what he was doing here. She was sure he'd come here to harm them, in one way or another.

'You're lying,' she said fiercely. 'I saw which direction you came from, Leó. I saw your tracks in the snow. You came past Anna's house and, if you really were looking for help, you'd have stopped there.'

'I . . . I don't remember seeing any other house, but then I was pretty far gone at the time. Maybe that's why I didn't notice it.'

'Did you knock on her door?'

'No, I came straight here. Is there any chance you . . . might have misinterpreted my footprints or something?' His gaze shifted to the window. 'Why don't we go out and check? Because I'm telling you the absolute truth.'

'Of course he's telling us the truth, Erla love,' Einar said. But she could hear from his voice that she had sown a seed of doubt in his mind. 'Why don't we turn the radio on again. We don't want to miss the Christmas greetings to friends and family.'

Erla ploughed on as if he hadn't spoken. 'It's far too late to go outside now, as well you know. All the tracks will have been buried under a fresh layer of snow. But there's only one road leading here and it goes past Anna's house, and I know . . . I know . . .'

At that moment the electricity went.

X

Hulda stood on the street corner in the raw winter weather, listening to a girls' choir vying with the wind to sing about Christmas, Christmas everywhere. The girls were all thickly wrapped up, as Hulda was herself, and seemed determined not to let the miserable weather spoil things. Hulda was carrying two shopping bags, containing a book and a record, both for Dimma. It was past 10 p.m. and the shops would soon be closing for the holiday.

She was alone. It wasn't how she had envisaged the evening. The plan had been to go out for a meal, then enjoy the festive atmosphere in town with Jón and Dimma, but nothing had come of it. Dimma had flatly refused to leave the house and once again locked herself in her room. Hulda and Jón had stood outside her door for a long time, trying to talk her round, arguing with her, even shouting at her, but nothing had worked. She wouldn't hear of going out.

'You go, Hulda love,' Jón had said at last. 'Relax, have

fun. I'll stay with Dimma. Go and buy her something nice from both of us.'

Hulda had hesitated before eventually giving in to his encouragement. Jón could be very persuasive. Besides, she reasoned to herself, the main purpose of going into town was to get something for Dimma. She would just have to try to make the best of a bad situation. This phase *had* to pass soon. Dimma was bound to be in a better, more cheerful frame of mind tomorrow. Back to her old happy, good-natured self.

Hulda walked up Laugavegur high street as if in a daze, trying but failing to get into the Christmas spirit. The jostling crowds pushed and shoved, and the dismal weather got on her nerves. Perhaps what the three of them needed was to get away, maybe even go abroad, somewhere warm and sunny. It might be worth discussing with Jón whether they could afford a holiday in the New Year, since, as far as she could gather, his business was going well. Perhaps a new environment would have a positive effect on Dimma and drag her out of her current downward spiral. And perhaps Hulda and Jón should work a bit less and devote more time to their daughter.

Hulda knew she got too engrossed in her job. But even as she acknowledged this, her thoughts returned to the missing girl, Unnur. The case she had failed to solve – so far, at least. It was almost certainly too late to save Unnur now, if it ever had been possible. But Hulda was troubled by niggling doubts about whether she had done enough. The police inspector in Selfoss had speculated about the possibility that the girl had got into a car with the wrong man and been attacked and murdered. If he was right, it meant her killer was still at large.

Hulda breathed in the chilly winter air and, turning on her heel, set off walking rapidly back down Laugavegur.

She had to try to get through to her daughter and help her pull herself out of this rut.

XI

Anna.

Erla thought about her as she lay there in the pitch-black bedroom, worrying that her daughter might not be able to walk over tomorrow if the weather was as bad as the forecast had said. She was still wide awake but could hear Einar snoring away at her side. He was always so untroubled; so different from her.

How could he sleep while that man was under their roof?

Leó – if that was his real name – had invaded the sanctuary of their home, and at Christmas too. The power cut had let him off the hook for now. There had been no point pursuing the conversation after the house had been plunged into darkness. Leó had been badly shaken – she could hear it in his voice – whereas she and Einar had reacted with prompt and practised ease, confident about where they could lay hands on candles and restore a little light to the sitting room. The upshot was that they had all retired to bed early. Once Einar had dropped off, she had got out of bed, tiptoed across the room and locked the door. They hadn't done that for years, but fortunately the key was left in the lock out of habit.

Although she had pulled the curtains to shut out the night, she could feel the snow building up relentlessly outside. When they first retired to bed, she had lit a candle on her bedside table and pretended to read an old Agatha Christie while Einar turned his back and went to sleep. She had read the book before and her thoughts were distracted, racing around in her head, incapable of focusing on the black letters on the white page. She had let the candle burn right down until it went out with a hiss of hot wax and darkness closed in around her. For all she knew, the power might have come back on by now, but she doubted it.

It was more likely that they would have to do without electricity for the whole of the Christmas holiday – it had happened before. But that didn't really matter; all that really mattered was getting that man out of their house and out of their lives.

Although she couldn't see anything, she could hear the wind and feel the cold sneaking in through the gaps in the window frame. The roaring of the gale was loud enough to keep those unaccustomed to it awake, but not her and Einar. It was such a frequent occurrence in this godforsaken spot that they were inured to the noise. She listened, doing her best to block out the weather and attune her ears to what was happening nearer at hand, trying to hear their visitor through the thin wooden partition wall, but as far as she could tell, everything was quiet indoors.

She lay there absolutely still, hardly breathing, alert to the faintest sound.

Lay on her back with her eyes wide open, staring blindly at the ceiling.

Sometimes, when she was going through one of her bad patches, she lay like this half the night or more, wondering if their life would have been better if they'd moved to Reykjavík; if Einar could have cut his damned umbilical cord and sold the farm, escaping the ancestral yoke. And sometimes, very occasionally, she let herself wonder if life would have been better if she'd never met Einar at all ... But the answer to that was more complicated, because without Einar there would have been no Anna. It was pointless brooding like this, but she did it anyway, the prisoner of her own memories, or rather the prisoner of her own mind.

There was another candle in the drawer of the bedside table. Erla reached for it now, groping for the matches in the darkness. She couldn't go on like this; she had to have a little light. She sat up in bed but, of course, Einar didn't stir. He slept the sleep of the carefree, of the self-contained. Erla struck a match, held it to the wick until it caught, then listened. Since there was no question of going to sleep, she resolved to wait it out.

But the tiredness was there underneath; however wide awake she was now, there was always a risk she might doze off. In an attempt to stave off drowsiness, she started thinking about her relatives in Reykjavík. She had little contact with them nowadays. Really, she was stuck in this marriage for the simple reason that she had nowhere else to turn. She wouldn't know what to do with herself if she ever left and moved back to the city. In spite of everything, she had put down roots here.

She emerged from this familiar train of thought to find herself still sitting up in bed. Closing her eyes, she listened to the silence indoors. Slowly, she became aware of the low humming of the house, which seemed to grow more insistent with every moment that passed. Then there was the rhythmic ticking of the alarm clock, so shockingly loud in the quietness, and seeming louder every minute. The roaring of the wind, the humming in the walls, the ticking of the clock, they all merged together until the noise grew unbearable, like a searing pain in her ears. She opened her eyes wide, trying to shake off the feeling.

And then she heard something.

Something real this time.

There was no mistaking it: somebody was moving around in the house.

Of course, there was only one person it could be. She heard the squeaking of a door, the muffled creaking of the floorboards. It was impossible to creep around noiselessly in this old house, but Leó was trying to do just that, and would probably have got away with it if Erla had been out for the count, like Einar.

Where was the bastard going?

She heard squeaking again, another door. Don't overreact, she told herself. He's probably just going to the toilet. But she could have sworn the noise came from the attic. Had he gone upstairs? For a moment she seriously considered tiptoeing out of their room and sneaking up on him to give him a shock. But she didn't have the guts. Although she knew the house like the back of her hand, had done her best to learn to recognize all its idiosyncratic noises and could find her way around it even with the lights off, this time the cause of her fear was a flesh-and-blood person. The last thing she wanted was to risk encountering him in the dark.

What she ought to do was wake Einar, but she hesitated, unsure how he would react. Besides, he might make a noise as he stirred, and there was a risk that would scare Leó back into his room.

Getting out of bed, she padded over to the door and listened, then turned the handle with infinite care to ensure that it was locked without making a betraying rattle. It was, of course. The certainty brought a rush of relief. She was safe in here.

All was quiet again. She couldn't hear anything to indicate that Leó was still moving around or to help her pinpoint his whereabouts, but in spite of that she was certain he'd left his room and hadn't yet returned to it. She stood motionless in the chilly bedroom, the shadows moving and dancing in the flickering candlelight, waiting. Every now and then she glanced back at the bed, where Einar was sleeping as if he hadn't a care in the world.

Then she heard it again. She pressed her ear to the door and, yes, she recognized that succession of creaks: Leó was descending the stairs from the attic; she was sure of it now. So she'd been right. His footsteps approached stealthily along the passage and her heart missed a beat.

She didn't know how long he had been snooping around the house but, as far as she was concerned, things had gone far enough. Without another thought, she walked softly over to the bed. As she did so, she heard more noises, the squeaking of a door, footsteps. She gave Einar a shove but he didn't immediately stir.

'Einar, Einar,' she whispered frantically, her breathing fast and shallow. 'You've got to wake up. Right now. Wake up!'

His eyes flicked open.

'It's Leó. I can hear him, Einar, I can hear him!'

Einar blinked, confused, and rubbed his eyes.

'Get up!' she hissed. 'Quietly.'

Obediently, he pushed back the covers and got out of bed. 'What's the matter, love?' he asked in a low voice. 'Why did you wake me?'

'You've got to stop him,' she hissed. 'It's Leó! He's prowling around the house – in the middle of the night!'

Einar went over to the door and took hold of the handle. 'It's locked,' he whispered, surprised. 'What the hell? Why's it locked?'

'*I* locked it. Because of him.' She went over to join her husband and softly turned the key so he could open it. He looked out into the passage, with Erla peering over his shoulder. There was nothing to see but darkness.

'Pass me the candle,' he said, gesturing back at the bedside table.

Erla did as he asked. Einar looked out of the door again, then ventured into the passage. She waited on tenterhooks in the bedroom.

He came almost straight back. 'There's no one there, love. You must have been dreaming. I expect the poor chap's sound asleep.'

She shook her head but didn't say anything.

'Come on, love. Let's try and go back to sleep ourselves. We don't want to be up and about in the middle of the night.' He closed the door but, to her chagrin, didn't lock it.

She went over and locked it herself, then got into bed next to him and turned over on her side, facing away from him, lying with her eyes stretched wide open.

XII

'Your mother's definitely coming over tomorrow, isn't she?' Jón asked from the armchair, without raising his eyes from his book. There was a sweet smell of cocoa in the air. He had heated milk for them and stirred in the best-quality drinking chocolate, but one of the three mugs was still standing untouched on the sofa table.

Hulda, who was engaged in the annual chore of trying to disentangle the fairy lights, answered curtly: 'Yes.' She would gladly have got out of the duty of hosting her mother for once and celebrated Christmas alone with Jón and Dimma. She was especially dreading her mother's visit this time, with Dimma being so difficult and unpredictable.

'I reckon we're all set,' Jón said, finally looking up from his book. 'Aren't we, darling?'

'Well, except for Dimma.'

'Oh, can't we talk about something else? Just leave her alone to get over it. She'll come round when it's time to open her presents.' He smiled at Hulda, but neither his smile nor his rallying tone rang true.

In the background they could hear the traditional Christmas messages to friends and family being read out over the radio, a reminder that this was the time of peace and harmony, but the emotions churning inside Hulda felt jarringly at odds with this spirit. She was anxious and upset. More than that, she felt apprehensive, though of what she didn't know.

'Do you *have* to work on Christmas Day?' Jón asked. 'Aren't you senior enough to have a bit more say in what shifts you get lumbered with these days?'

'I can't do anything about it; it's just how the rota worked out. Is it a problem?'

'No, of course not. It's fine. Dimma and I will just read our books while you're out. Maybe we could do a puzzle too. We've got an old jigsaw in the loft, haven't we?'

'Several, yes.'

'Then we'll have a nice lazy time. Like in the old days before Dimma was born, when it was just you and me. Do you remember how we used to snuggle up on the sofa and read for days on end over Christmas and Easter? With no one to disturb us.'

'Yes, before you started working so much.'

He smiled. She knew that smile. It was his way of defusing difficult conversations, and she'd fallen for it every time. Ever since they first got together.

'You'll take good care of her while I'm out, won't you?' she asked, a pleading note in her voice.

'On Christmas Day? Of course I will.'

'Promise me, Jón,' she said.

XIII

Erla started awake and automatically reached for the alarm clock, peering at the hands in the gloom. It was morning, gone seven o'clock. She must have fallen asleep in spite of herself. The disturbances of the night felt like a bad dream. Could she have imagined it, or part of it, at least? Suddenly she wasn't sure . . . not entirely, and the thought unsettled her.

After a moment she registered that Einar was no longer lying by her side. She sat up and tried to switch on the light, but nothing happened: the power was obviously still out. The morning was pitch black, as usual at this time of year, indistinguishable from the night, but the clock didn't lie. She felt a momentary stab of fear. Could something have happened to Einar? Closing her eyes, she listened, but couldn't hear anything. All was quiet in the house.

Too quiet?

Her heart began to race, making the blood throb in her head, and next minute she was out of bed and running into the passage in her nightclothes. It was lighter out there than in the bedroom, illuminated by a dim glow that appeared to be coming from the sitting room. Heading towards it, she found the room lit up by candles and Einar and the man who called himself Leó both sitting there.

There was a comforting aroma of coffee in the air. Then her gaze alighted on the tree and the colourful parcels beneath it and it dawned on her that it was Christmas Eve.

'You're awake, love,' Einar said. 'There's hot coffee in the pot. Thank God, the gas is still working.'

She stood rooted to the spot, the words stuck in her throat. The seconds seemed to be passing as slowly as minutes as she stood there, speechless, feeling the weight of the men's stares bearing down on her.

She opened her mouth, but no words came out.

'Why don't you join us?' Einar asked.

'Anna?' she croaked at last. 'Isn't she here yet?'

'I thought the road was blocked?' Leó muttered, avoiding Erla's eye.

'You can always get through on foot,' Erla contradicted him sharply. 'What's the weather like now?'

She glanced at the window, but all she could see was the reflection of the candles.

'Sit down, love,' Einar said. 'I didn't want to wake you.'

Instead of obeying, she turned and went into the hall.

'You had such a disturbed night,' Einar called after her. 'I thought I should let you lie in a bit. This power cut really seems to have got to you.'

'I'm perfectly used to power cuts,' she retorted from

the hall. She opened the front door and stuck her head out into the unrelieved darkness, then took a step forward in her thick socks, hardly knowing what she was doing, and sank straight into a deep, fresh snowdrift. Icy flakes brushed against her face. She jerked back her foot, feeling the cold biting through flesh and bone. What an incredibly stupid thing to do, wading out into the snow like that.

She retreated into the hall and closed the door.

'What on earth were you thinking, Erla?' Einar boomed in her ear, laying a hand on her shoulder.

She was so shocked she almost lost her balance.

'Is everything all right?' he asked, concerned.

The blood was throbbing in her head again. She rubbed her temples and tried to concentrate. It was safe to say that she had got out of bed on the wrong side. She would have to pull herself together. After all, she thought with a sudden sense of relief, they had got through the night unharmed, and Leó would be leaving shortly.

Turning to her husband, she said in a falsely cheerful tone: 'Yes, of course everything's all right. I was just going to check on the weather and accidentally stepped in some snow. It's very deep out there.'

'It's been falling all night, love. Come back in and have some coffee.'

She followed Einar into the sitting room and sat down in an armchair, waiting while he fetched her a cup, uncomfortably conscious of her wet sock. She didn't say a word and deliberately avoided looking at Leó, who was still sitting on the sofa, facing her across the coffee table, nursing his cup and raising it to his lips from time to time.

Only when Einar came back and took the chair next to her did she find her voice. 'Still no electricity?' she asked her husband in a low voice.

She knew there wasn't but had felt compelled to break the silence somehow. Anyway, there was a certain comfort in asking a question to which you already knew the answer.

'It'll be out all bloody Christmas, I guarantee you,' said Einar.

'Do you get used to this?' Leó asked with a smile.

The room was illuminated by five candles, three on the table, two on the sideboard, the jerky shadows making the familiar surroundings appear oddly eerie. Erla felt almost as if she were trapped in a bad dream.

'Yes, you get used to it,' she said after a delay, then added, with an edge: 'But you needn't worry about that, since you'll be leaving as soon as you've finished your coffee. Has Einar gone over the route with you?'

Instead of answering, Leó threw a glance at Einar, and for a while there was an embarrassed silence, as if the two men had formed an alliance from which she was excluded.

Einar cleared his throat. 'I don't think he'll be going anywhere today.'

'Not going anywhere? What do you mean?'

'You saw for yourself, love: the snow's too deep. There's a storm out there. We can't send the poor man out in that.' From the way he spoke, Einar might have been talking about someone who wasn't present, rather than about the man who was sitting right in front of them.

'Of course he can go!' Erla tried to stop her voice rising to a screech. 'If Anna can get here, he must be able to leave, even if he does have a bit further to go.'

'Your husband tells me it's actually quite a long –'

'And why didn't you tell us you'd stopped off at Anna's place first?' Erla interrupted him. 'Did you meet her? Hm? Did you meet her?'

'I didn't meet anyone on my way here, not a soul,' Leó assured her, looking uneasy now. 'That's the honest truth.'

'Why don't you go back to bed, love?' Einar said gently. 'You're tired. Leó's spending Christmas with us, and that's all there is to it. We can't just throw him out in weather like this.'

Erla groaned. She felt as if the walls were closing in on her, as if she were alone in the world, with no allies. And she was worried sick about Anna. She became conscious of her quickened breathing. The desperation to speak, to convey her fears to Einar, was so intense that it almost choked her.

Leó stood up. 'Look, I think I'll go back to my room. I do apologize for the inconvenience. I'm really very sorry. And very grateful for your hospitality – you must know that.'

Einar nodded, but didn't say anything.

Only when Leó had left the room did Erla calm down enough to speak. 'Einar . . .' She struggled to find the words to express her fears. 'Einar, you know he's lying to us.'

'We shouldn't always believe the worst of people, Erla.'

'But why didn't they mention it on the news?'

'Perhaps they did, love. We haven't been able to listen to the radio since the electricity went. Perhaps there's a search party out looking for him even as we speak.'

'You know perfectly well there isn't. And his tracks – he came along the road, past Anna's house. He's lying that he stumbled on our place by chance. And . . . and . . .' Again she felt the pressure building up in her temples, the beginnings of a splitting headache. 'And he was snooping around last night, and yesterday too, when we weren't there to see. He wants something from us, Einar. I saw him, he was in *our bedroom* yesterday. And last night – I don't know where – up in the attic maybe, or in the sitting room. I don't know, Einar, all I know is that he . . . that he . . .'

'Come on, let's get you back to bed, love,' he said kindly. 'You need a rest.'

XIV

Hulda knocked on the door again, a prolonged, hard rapping.

'Why are you behaving like this, Dimma?' she shouted, her throat constricting with unshed tears and frustration.

From inside the room she could hear some kind of response but couldn't make out the words. Dimma had emerged that morning and eaten her breakfast in silence, not even returning her parents' 'good morning'.

Hulda had suggested that she and Dimma should wrap up their presents together or at least drive round and drop off those that needed to be delivered, but Dimma had merely shaken her head to whatever suggestion she made. It seemed to mean nothing to her that it was Christmas Eve. She had withdrawn so entirely into her own little world that nothing outside it appeared to matter to her.

Hulda had been so sure that everything would improve once Christmas arrived, but it was all too clear that there would be no seasonal good cheer in their house. Only now, belatedly, had it sunk in: she couldn't just stand by any more, she would have to intervene.

She had found it difficult to admit the situation to herself and face up to the fact that their daughter needed professional help, but she was at her wits' end. And Jón was no use. She carried on furiously banging on her daughter's door, although she knew it wouldn't do any good. Her anger was mainly directed at herself for not having acted sooner. She had gone on deluding herself that Dimma would snap out of it, but it was obvious now that there was no hope of that.

'Come out, Dimma, come out right now!' she shouted. 'Or . . . or we'll break the door down. I'm not joking.'

Jón grabbed her hard by the shoulders. 'Calm down, Hulda. She'll get over –'

'She won't get over it, Jón!' Hulda yelled, rounding on her husband. 'She won't bloody well get over it. She's had plenty of chances. No one behaves like this.'

'Come on, come back to the sitting room; you've got to calm down.'

'I have no intention of calming down. We've got to get her . . . get her to a doctor.' Hulda's voice broke and, once the floodgates had opened, she found herself sobbing uncontrollably, hardly able to stammer out the words.

Jón pulled her gently but firmly away from the door and guided her into the sitting room. Hulda fought him at first, but eventually gave in, feeling utterly defeated.

'Jón,' she cried, 'we have to get an appointment for her . . . with a therapist, a psychiatrist . . . we have to do something.'

'Isn't that a bit drastic, Hulda, love?' he said, his voice soothing. 'There's no need to blow this up out of all proportion.'

'Out of all proportion? Are you completely blind, Jón? Deliberately blind? There's something seriously wrong and we should have realized it a long time ago. Perhaps there's a problem at school? Something . . . I mean, what's happened to all her friends? She doesn't seem to have any left.'

'Darling, let's wait and see until after Christmas. I know you were hoping she'd come round and things would be like they used to be, but we have to accept that it's not going to happen. Let's just take a deep breath and let her lock herself in her room if she wants to. Perhaps she just needs to be alone. What do we know about it?'

'But that's exactly what I mean! What do we know about what's going on in her head? Nothing! That's why we need professional help. I want us to ring someone now, today!'

'It's Christmas Eve. We're not ringing anybody, Hulda. Forget it. Everyone will be on holiday. I promise we'll talk to someone between Christmas and New Year, if she hasn't snapped out of it by then. OK?'

Hulda thought about it, her chest heaving with suppressed sobs. Although she didn't agree that they should wait, she had to admit there was something in what Jón said. They could hardly justify calling out a doctor or a child psychologist during a public holiday unless it was an emergency. Perhaps she was overreacting.

'We'll see,' she answered grudgingly. It was all she would say for now.

The worst part was that she had to go into work tomorrow, on the twenty-fifth. It was incredibly unfortunate that her shifts should have fallen out like that, and of course Jón was right in a way that she had been with the police long enough to be able to refuse to work on major holidays. But the truth was that she didn't dare say no: her life in the police was a perpetual battle with the patriarchy and she felt compelled to do more than was expected of her, however much she might regret the fact now.

In fact, damn it, why should she have to take the shift? She would just tell them to find someone else. She rushed out into the hall, snatched up the phone and rang her colleague, who was on duty.

'Hello, Hulda here . . .' Even as she spoke, she realized it was a stupid idea; there wouldn't be anyone in CID today except this officer, who had no power to release her from tomorrow's shift.

'Hello, everything OK?'

'What, oh, yes, sure . . . Are you the only person on duty today?'

'Of course. People aren't exactly queuing up to come in on Christmas Eve. It's a hell of a bummer to get landed with this shift. I'm hoping I'll make it home early this evening, though, if things stay this quiet.'

'Is . . . er, I don't suppose there's any chance you could take my shift for me tomorrow?'

There was a brief silence at the other end, then he burst out laughing. 'Nice one, Hulda! The answer is no – no chance.'

'Do you . . . is there anyone . . . The thing is, I've got a bit of a problem at home,' she persisted, trying to stop her voice from wobbling.

'You haven't got a hope in hell of getting someone else to take your shift at such short notice. You'll just have to come in tomorrow and find some other way to solve the problem at home.'

'Yes, I . . . suppose . . .'

'Listen, while I remember, there was a message for you when I arrived this morning. Someone on the switchboard took it down.'

'A message?'

'Yes, that you should ring some number, hang on . . . six-five-six something, I can't remember the rest. Just a sec.'

Hulda wanted to hang up; she had absolutely no interest in dealing with work matters today, but she waited in spite of herself. Finally, her colleague located the phone number, but the message had apparently contained no other information.

'Could you look it up for me?' she asked. 'I can't think whose number it is.'

'Yes, sure, of course. It's not as if I've got much else to do. Give me a minute.' There was a rustling as he put down the receiver. After a short interval he picked it up again: 'It's a Gardabær number, Kolbrún and Haukur –'

'Oh, right, them . . .' She wondered why on earth they had been trying to get hold of her. 'When did they call?'

'It doesn't say. Could have been yesterday evening, or maybe this morning. When did you leave work?'

'Yesterday afternoon . . . Right, OK, I'll . . . I'll ring them.'

The parents of the girl who had vanished . . . The case that had been so much on her mind recently. Perhaps they wanted to know how matters stood, before everything shut down for the holiday.

Hulda considered returning their call then and there, but she couldn't bring herself to. She had enough to cope with at home. Instead, she decided to put it off until she was at work tomorrow, since it seemed she had no alternative but to go into the office.

XV

When Erla resurfaced, after going back to bed at her husband's suggestion, her first thought was a fervent prayer that the events of the morning had been nothing but a long, unsettling dream; that Leó had finally left and Anna had arrived, so that Christmas could begin in earnest.

To distract herself, she focused on the ordinary household chores she needed to do before evening, like getting dinner ready, which would mean boiling the smoked lamb on the gas cooker and making sure the house was spick and span by 6 p.m., when the Icelandic Christmas celebrations traditionally began. She found herself smiling in anticipation, but her smile faded when she remembered the power cut. What a nuisance: they would miss the carol service this year. They did have a battery-run transistor, but it had stopped working ages ago and Einar had never got round to taking it in to be fixed. At the time he had said he'd gladly do without news for a few days the next time they had a power cut: 'It's nothing but doom and gloom anyway. We're better off without it.'

The sound of Leó's voice from the sitting room broke into her happy daydream and brought her crashing down to earth.

'Hell,' she muttered to herself, and checked the alarm clock. She had slept to midday. She couldn't remember the last time she'd done that. It must be because she'd lain awake so long last night.

Anna. Surely Anna must be here by now. She always got here by lunchtime, Erla thought to herself, smiling again. And with Anna there to back her up, perhaps Erla would survive Leó's visit after all.

She climbed out of bed, pulled on some clothes and made her way slowly along the passage to the sitting room. There they sat, Einar and Leó, as if they hadn't stirred since this morning. They had blown out the candles, and a pale, watery light was filtering in through the windows. Dawn, such as it was in winter, had broken, and it made sense to spare the candles and make the most of whatever daylight they got, since the darkness would close in again in just over three hours' time. It had stopped snowing, thank God, so perhaps they would be able to get shot of Leó after all.

'Where's Anna?' she asked.

She was met by silence. Leó dropped his eyes, avoiding her gaze.

'Why isn't Anna here? It's lunchtime, Einar. She should be here by now.'

Einar rose to his feet. 'It's all right, love. Come and sit down; I'll get some coffee.'

He went into the kitchen and came back with a cup, which he put on the table and filled with coffee. She felt as if the morning was repeating itself, as if she were caught in some sort of nightmarish loop.

'It's not all right, Einar. It's Christmas Eve, and she's never been this late before. And there you are, behaving as if nothing was wrong!' Erla made a sudden move towards him and gave him a shove. 'What's the matter with you? Why are you being like this?' Even as she said it, she realized she was taking out her anger on the wrong man. She had only one ally here and that was her husband. She rounded on Leó instead.

'It's time you stopped lying to us, Leó!' she said aggressively, taking a step towards him. He looked alarmed – the bastard was actually frightened of her! Serve him right.

'I . . . I'm not lying,' he stammered.

She went over and sat down on the sofa beside him, although there wasn't much room. She was going to get the truth out of him, whatever it took.

'You claimed you found our house by chance, didn't you?'

'Yes, thank God . . . I reckon it saved my life,' he faltered.

He was nervous, there was no question of it.

'You're lying. That's a lie. I saw your tracks in the snow. You followed the road here. Oh, yes, you told us that – that there were markers in the snow and you followed them.' She was astonished at how firm she sounded, at the courage she was able to summon up now that the chips were down. But there was a cold, sinking fear in the pit of her stomach. She was afraid for her daughter, afraid that this intruder might have hurt Anna in some way.

Leó was silent.

'That's what you told us yesterday, isn't it?'

'Yes, er, sure, but I didn't mean it like . . . I saw some markers, that's right, but . . .'

'And they lead here, but first they go past Anna's house. The road comes up from the village. And that's where you came from. You weren't out shooting on the moors with your friends – whether there were two or three of them, or however many it is today!' The thought that she might be fighting for her daughter's life lent her an unaccustomed strength. For God's sake, Anna should have been here by now!

'I *was* shooting,' Leó contradicted her, more forcefully this time. 'We were, er, shooting ptarmigan.'

Einar finally intervened. 'Where's your gun, then, mate?' he asked quietly, a hint of steel in his voice.

At last, at last, Erla thought, he was beginning to see the light. He'd realized there was something wrong.

'My gun? Oh, my gun. I, er, I dumped it when I got separated from the others. I was getting tired and didn't want to weigh myself down with unnecessary clobber.'

Erla held back, leaving it to Einar to treat this explanation with the contempt it deserved.

But Einar didn't immediately respond and a fraught silence descended on the little room. The atmosphere was peculiar enough anyway, thanks to the power cut; a sort of twilit gloom prevailed, evoking the time of day that Erla always found most sinister: the hour when ghosts could emerge from the shadows and take on human form, without your being any the wiser.

She shuddered; it was chilly in the room, as usual, but it wasn't this that triggered her reaction so much as a fervent wish that this stranger had never turned up on their doorstep, never disturbed the precarious balance of their home life. Yes, she was unhappy here – in a way; she couldn't lie to herself, but she longed to be left in peace with her unhappiness.

She strained her ears, listening out for the sound of the door opening that would herald Anna's arrival. Waiting for her to breeze into the room, her hair still crusted with snow from her walk, full of apologies for being so late. Once she was here, there would be no need to interrogate Leó. Because maybe, just maybe, he was telling the truth. Her confidence wavered, but then she reminded herself that he could be lying to cover up the fact that he had done something to Anna.

'So you left your gun behind, did you, mate?' Einar asked at last, in a deceptively level voice.

Leó nodded, his eyes darting from side to side as if it was dawning on him that the game was up and he had lost. That he wasn't welcome here any more.

'Yes,' he said after a brief hesitation.

'That strikes me as a bit of an odd thing to do. Guns are expensive toys – they cost an arm and a leg, as I'm sure you're aware. I've never heard of anyone dumping their gun like that. Do you have any idea where you left it? Did you mark the spot?'

'No, not really. Anyway, I didn't have anything to mark it with.'

'You're obviously not short of money, then.'

'What? No, of course I'm upset about the cost. I suppose the truth is I panicked – I was scared I was going to die of exposure out there.'

'And you came up the road, you say. Didn't you notice the other house on the way here?'

There was a long pause.

'The other house?' Leó asked hesitantly.

'Yes, my wife was asking you about that last night, and again this morning.'

'Oh, right, yes . . .'

'You said you hadn't seen any buildings apart from our place, but there's another house that belongs to us too, not that far off. The road from the village runs right past it.' Einar sounded unusually stern.

Leó didn't reply.

'So you didn't follow the road? The markers?'

'Yes . . . er, yes, I did.'

'And yet you didn't see the house. Or was it our place you were looking for?'

The silence stretched out, heavy with tension. Einar had drawn back slightly, as if to put more distance between himself and Leó, and Erla leaned as far away from their visitor as she could, as if to underline the fact that it was two against one and he was on his own.

'Look,' Leó said, on the defensive now, 'it's possible I saw it. I . . . I did see a building in the distance, but all the lights were off, so I just kept going. It could have been the house you're talking about, but I was knackered and feeling the cold so badly by then . . . I was looking out for signs of life, for a light –'

'It's our daughter's house,' Erla cut in, 'and there's no way she'd have refused you shelter if you'd knocked at her door. Do you know what I think?' – she raised her voice – 'I think you did go there and she took you in, and . . . and then you did something to her. That's what I think! She's not here yet, she still hasn't turned up . . . Tell us the truth, Leó. For God's sake, you have to tell us the truth!'

'Erla . . .' Einar intervened. 'Erla, love . . .'

'I swear I didn't meet her, I didn't even knock at the door – the house looked . . . there were no lights on that I could see. I really don't know what I was thinking. It's hard to think straight in a situation like that.'

Einar abruptly took a step closer to Leó and raised his voice: 'What do you want from us?'

'What . . . what do I want from you? Nothing, I just needed shelter. This is all some kind of terrible misunderstanding.'

'What have you done to Anna?' Erla cried, feeling the tears sliding down her cheeks. 'What have you done to her?'

'I've never met Anna, I swear to you . . .'

'My wife tells me you were snooping around in our bedroom yesterday,' Einar said, keeping up the relentless inquisition. 'Is that true?'

Leó was visibly thrown by the accusation. 'No. No, I don't know why she'd think that.'

'I *saw* you when I came in. I'm positive,' Erla said flatly.

'You saw me in the corridor, you mean. You must be imagining things,' Leó shot back.

'Let's just watch what we say here,' Einar said steadily,

but still with that steel in his voice. 'It's possible my wife made a mistake, but it seems to me there are a number of things that need explaining.'

'I don't know what to say,' their visitor protested with a sigh. 'I haven't lied about anything and I don't understand why you're accusing me like this. If you don't want me here, I'll leave right now.'

'Just hold your horses. No one's saying that,' Einar told him. 'We just want you to be straight with us.'

'But I *have* been straight with –'

Erla jumped in again: 'What about last night? What were you doing prowling around?' Even as she said it, she experienced a momentary doubt, wondering if it had been a dream. Maybe she hadn't actually heard the stealthy noises or the squeaking of the door in the attic. But when she saw the faint twitch of a muscle in Leó's cheek, the infinitesimal widening of his eyes, she knew it hadn't been her imagination. She threw a quick glance at her husband and saw that he had caught it as well, the betraying signs of guilt.

Leó sat there in silence.

'I heard you, you went up to the attic.'

'How on earth –?'

'. . . do I know that? Because I know this house.'

'So, yet more questions for you to answer, Leó.'

'I . . .' their visitor said, and stalled. Erla sensed that he was trying to make up his mind whether to keep lying to them or to admit the truth. 'All right,' he went on, 'as a matter of fact I was up and about last night. I couldn't sleep. I was feeling a bit claustrophobic, to be honest. I'm not used to being snowed in like this. I put my head out of the door for a breath of air, but it didn't help, just made me even more aware than before of how . . . well, how isolated this place is.'

'And the attic? What were you doing up there? And don't bother lying to me, Leó – I heard you open the door up there.' She added for good measure: 'And so did my husband.'

'Oh, I don't really know what I wanted. I just thought I'd try the bed up there, see if I'd feel any less claustrophobic upstairs . . .'

Einar walked over to the sofa and laid a heavy hand on Leó's shoulder. 'And how did that work out, mate? Did you go back to the spare room after that?' There was a warning note in his voice.

Leó lowered his eyes, answering after a moment or two: 'Yes, I managed to get to sleep in the end. I'm sorry if I kept you two awake.'

'Come along,' Einar said. It was an order, but a polite one. His hand was still resting on the guest's shoulder.

'Where? What do you mean?'

'Come upstairs.'

'Up . . . to the attic?'

'Yes, come with me. I just want to make sure nothing's been damaged or stolen,' Einar said firmly, adding, when Leó didn't react: 'Unless you'd rather I didn't check?'

'No, of course not. I've nothing to hide.'

'Right, then, let's go upstairs. You lead – after all, you already know the way.'

Erla saw the confusion in Leó's eyes, but he obeyed

and walked slowly up the stairs in front of Einar. The door to the attic room was locked from the outside and, when Erla heard the squeak of the key, she realized that this had almost certainly been the noise she had picked up on last night.

'Ah, it's dark up here, of course,' she heard Einar say. 'The window's covered with snow. Hang on a minute. I'm going to fetch a candle.'

Erla jumped when she heard the sound of the door shutting and the key turning in the lock. The seconds seemed to pass as slowly as minutes while it gradually dawned on her that her husband had locked their guest in.

Then she heard the first shouts. 'What the fuck's going on?' Leó's voice carried clearly down to where she was standing. He shook the handle, then started banging on the door, but Erla knew it wouldn't give way that easily. This was a solid old house and most of the doors were correspondingly thick and sturdy. 'Let me out, for fuck's sake! Let me out! This is against the law. Let me out!' He started pounding on the door again.

Einar came downstairs, looking unperturbed.

'Right, love, let's take a quick look through his things. I'm not quite sure about this fellow. I think you might have been right about him all along.'

He called back over his shoulder: 'Just be patient a minute, mate. I'll be back shortly.'

Erla could hardly believe what had just happened, relieved though she was that Einar had apparently decided to take her fears seriously. 'What are you doing?' she whispered, going over to him.

'There's something fishy about all this, love. Let's find out if he's telling the truth.'

'But what . . . what are you going to do? Are you planning to keep him locked up . . . right through Christmas?'

'No, of course not,' Einar replied, as Leó kept up his violent assault on the door upstairs. 'That wouldn't do. Besides, this may all turn out to be a big misunderstanding, in which case we'll let him out at once. But we need to be careful. I'm not putting you at risk from some stranger.'

'But what –?'

'I'm just going to take a look through his things. I'll soon see if he's been lying to us.' He shook his head and snorted contemptuously: 'Going shooting without a gun, can you beat that?'

Had that been the tipping point? Little by little, the clues that something wasn't quite right had been piling up. But maybe Einar had only started putting two and two together now, because this was something he knew about, as a keen hunter who had shot quite a few ptarmigan himself that winter – that no real hunter would have left his gun behind.

Einar's gun . . . Suddenly Erla had a horrible thought. 'Einar,' she whispered, 'your gun! Could he have broken into the cabinet last night? Could that have been what he was looking for?'

Her husband frowned. 'It's locked, and I always keep the key on me, you know that.' He patted his pocket. 'Still, that's a good point. I'll go and check.'

He disappeared down the passage and returned shortly afterwards, shaking his head. 'No, the gun's still in the cabinet and there's no sign that anyone's tried to tamper with the lock. Right, let's have a look at his things.'

Erla stood, rigid, watching as he went into the spare room, and suddenly, incongruously, found herself thinking about the smoked lamb. To distract herself, she started trying to work out what time she would need to put it on to boil and when she would have to start on the side dishes to accompany it. Christmas dinner was the most important meal of the year and it always required a countdown to make sure everything went smoothly. They normally had a light snack at midday too, but it had completely escaped her mind in all the fuss.

She closed her eyes, trying to block out the hammering and yelling from upstairs and focus on these mundane concerns, as if they could transport her to another world where all was well. Where the light hadn't fled before the darkness of a power cut; where no visitor had turned up unexpectedly out of the snow; where Christmas carols were playing softly on the stereo in the background; where only the familiar phantoms went on the prowl at night and not a sinister stranger, and where Anna had turned up to lunch on Christmas Eve . . .

Anna?

The thought of Anna jolted Erla out of her daydreams and back into the harsh present. There was still no sign of their daughter.

XVI

Hulda's mother was comfortably ensconced on the sofa with a glass of malt brew. She said little, but every now and then helped herself to a chocolate from the bowl on the coffee table. Hulda had done her best to pretend everything was fine. On the radio in the background, greetings were being read out from the families of fishermen who were away at sea over the holiday.

'Apparently it's an extra-long Christmas this year,' Hulda's mother announced, apropos of nothing.

'Extra long?'

'Yes, someone was talking about it on the radio yesterday. When Christmas falls just before a Sunday, you get an extra-long holiday.' Her smile seemed strained. She was habitually tired and always had been, as far back as Hulda could remember; always on the go, trying to make ends meet, trying to hold down several jobs simultaneously. Even now that she was approaching retirement, she still worked from morning to night, cleaning houses.

Hulda had promised herself many times that she wasn't going to end up like that when she was her mother's age. On the contrary, she was determined that by then she and Jón would be debt free and sufficiently well off to be able to give up work at a reasonable age and make the most of their retirement.

Jón was nowhere to be seen; he'd retreated into his study, claiming there was some urgent business he needed to tie up before Christmas. It got on Hulda's nerves that he chose to work such long hours, despite being his own boss, but she couldn't really complain when it meant they had such a comfortable lifestyle. There were times, though, like now, when she suspected it was nothing but an excuse to avoid having to spend too much time with his mother-in-law.

Hulda forced herself to keep her mother company in the sitting room, though they had little to say to each other and any conversation they did have wasn't usually initiated by her.

'Are we going to listen to the carol service later?'

'Yes, Mum, during supper, as usual.'

'I just wanted to make sure. It feels right somehow. Puts you in the Christmas spirit.' After a brief silence, she added: 'Are we having the usual gammon this evening?'

'Yes, Mum, we're not doing anything different from usual.'

'Oh, good, that's lovely. Not what I was brought up with, but lovely all the same . . . By the way, where's Dimma?'

'She's resting, Mum. You know what teenagers are like . . .'

'Oh. I've got two presents for my darling girl.' She lowered her voice: 'A jumper I knitted myself and a book. I do hope she'll like them.'

Hulda nodded dutifully. 'I'm sure she will, Mum. I'm sure she will.'

XVII

Erla hung back and let Einar go alone into the spare room to search Leó's luggage. She waited, caught between hope and fear, still trying to block out the banging and shouting from upstairs.

Now that Einar was acting on her suspicions, she suddenly started having second thoughts. Supposing she had misread the situation and Leó hadn't been lying to them after all? He could indeed have got lost and muddled up a few details because he was in a bad state after his ordeal.

Oh God, she thought, if that was true, what would happen? He was bound to report them to the police the moment he got back to the village. They might even find themselves facing criminal charges ... She could feel herself breathing faster. No, stop being silly, she told herself: they could simply deny everything. It was the only way. It would be his word against theirs.

No, I have absolutely no idea what the man's talking about. We took him in and offered him a room for the night, and this is how he repays us!

Mentally, she rehearsed the conversation with the police, trying to envisage which officer would come to see them. The inspector, perhaps? Yes, probably. A middle-aged man who she'd never much cared for.

'Erla! Come here!' Einar's shout penetrated the mist that surrounded her. 'Come and see what I've found!'

Apprehensively, she started towards the spare room, feeling her heart fluttering against her ribcage.

'Hurry up.'

She peered round the door and saw Einar holding up a compass with a look of triumph.

'He did have a compass, the lying bastard. So he can't have been all that lost. Which means he lied to us about having no idea which way he was going. You know, I wouldn't be surprised if he sabotaged the phone line as well. If you ask me, it's a bit bloody suspicious that the line went down right about the time he turned up.'

'Do you think . . . Are you serious?' Actually, Einar's theory wasn't that far-fetched. The phone had been working fine the day before Leó arrived and the line usually held out whatever the weather, even when the electricity went.

'We'd better take a look at it. I'm no telephone engineer, but I'm going to check it out anyway.' Einar went on rooting around in the visitor's rucksack.

Erla retreated a few steps. She stood there, slightly stunned, watching her husband behaving as if he'd been seized by a fit of madness, shaking the rucksack and roughly pulling the contents out of it.

Einar was normally a placid man, but she had seen this

side of him before. Not often, but a handful of times; enough to know what he was capable of. Luckily, he'd never taken his temper out on her. No, he'd always treated her well, but when he felt he'd been pushed too far, he could fly into terrifying rages. It wasn't an exaggeration to say that he turned into a completely different person.

'Hey, look at this, Erla!' Einar held up a wad of five-thousand-krónur notes. 'Cash, lots of it. You were right, his story doesn't add up.'

Erla's mind flew to Anna again. The man had lied to them, repeatedly. 'All right, go on looking,' she said. 'But God help us if we're wrong, Einar. God help us.'

The blows on the door upstairs were violent enough to shake the house. 'Open the door this minute!' Leó bellowed. 'You can't do this to me!'

XVIII

'Erla, come back. You have to see this!' Einar shouted urgently. She was poised in the doorway, unable to move, wishing with all her heart that she was somewhere else. Anywhere but here, caught up in this awful situation.

What if she gave up now, slipped out of the house and ran away, in no particular direction, just to escape? But she knew it was no good. She felt suffocated by the oppressive weight of the snow surrounding them and shutting them in.

At this time of year, in this weather, there was no way out.

However loudly she screamed, however fast she ran, all she could look forward to was a slow death from hypothermia. It was no wonder she often thought of their home as a prison.

'Erla, are you listening? Come here.'

'I heard you,' she said, controlling her voice. 'But I don't want to come in, Einar. I don't want any part in this. It . . . it feels wrong. We're committing a crime against this man. We can't keep him locked up like this. We have to let him out.'

'But you were the one who was scared of him, Erla! Not me. You know, sometimes I don't understand you. You've got to stop this nonsense. This is real, Erla, this is what reality is like. This man is real, and I reckon he's got something to hide. In fact, I'm sure of it. And *this* is proof!' He was brandishing a battered wallet.

'I'm *not* coming in!' Erla shrieked, feeling herself starting to shake.

'Well, then, take a look at this.' He opened the wallet and held it up towards her. She took a wary step into the room, as if trespassing in a stranger's house. Obediently, she examined the man's ID.

'Look at his driving licence,' Einar said. 'The picture's of him but Leó's only a middle name. It's like he didn't want to tell us his real name.'

'Maybe he goes by his middle name,' Erla countered. She wasn't sure what to think. She'd been racked by doubts ever since Leó arrived. 'What's going on, Einar?' she asked, her voice trembling.

'I don't know, love, but I'm going to find out.' He sounded tough, determined. In a way, Erla was relieved that Einar had taken the matter in hand, but at the same time she couldn't help feeling apprehensive. When he lost his temper like this, there was a danger he'd do something rash.

Grabbing the rucksack, he upended it, tipping the rest of the contents out in a heap on the floor – clothes, toiletries: nothing immediately suspicious. Einar shook the bag, then peered inside it. 'Empty. We'll have to go through his stuff; see if we can find any clues about who he is and what he's up to. For all we know, he could be a criminal on the run.'

'You don't think he'll break the door down, do you?' she asked.

'I hope not, but if he does, I'll deal with him. I'm not scared of a wimpy city boy. I reckon I could take him.' Erla had no doubt he could. Einar was powerfully built, as if he had inherited the accumulated energy of all his forefathers, who had fought such a bitter battle against the elements to keep this remote patch of land inhabited. They had been successful right up to the present day, but now the omens were gathering, suggesting that the farm's days were numbered, as was obvious to everyone except Einar himself. If only they could move away . . . set up home somewhere else. But Erla knew it wasn't that simple. All their worldly goods were more or less tied up in the property: the farming business, the equipment, the livestock . . . It would be no easy matter to sell them. An old house far from the nearest village was worthless if no one wanted to live there. All the derelict properties scattered around the Icelandic countryside bore silent witness to this fact, and Erla could picture the same fate befalling their own house once they'd moved away: broken windows, flaking paint, rusty corrugated-iron roof; an empty husk, no longer a home, fit for no one but the ghosts that roamed the wastes.

Admittedly, they owned the land too, a sizeable property, but the same applied to that as to the house; an estate in this area wasn't worth a bean except to the farmer who was prepared to live out here. It would never be popular as a summer-house colony, not with its savage winters and chilly summers.

While her thoughts slipped into this well-worn groove, Einar had been rummaging around in the contents of the backpack. 'Nothing of interest here.'

'What about that pocket?' she asked.

'What? Where?' he asked eagerly.

'On the side, there.' Erla pointed to a deep pocket on the side of the rucksack.

'Oh, yes, well spotted. Maybe he's got something hidden in there.' Einar undid the zip and reached inside. 'What the —?'

XIX

Einar pulled a hunting knife out of the pocket.

Drawing it from its sheath, he tested the blade with his thumb. 'It's bloody sharp too.'

Erla stiffened with fear. She realized it was vital to calm him down. She knew her husband in this mood; that expression, the ominous note in his voice.

'There could be a perfectly natural explanation for it, dear. The man was on a shooting trip, after all.'

'Shooting ptarmigan with a knife?'

'There's nothing odd about taking a knife along on a shooting trip – as a safety precaution.' But her husband wasn't listening.

'I reckon it's time to have a word with him,' he said grimly, making for the door.

Erla blocked his path. 'Einar . . . Einar.'

'Let me go and talk to him, Erla.' He was still holding the knife.

'Put the knife down, Einar.'

'I'm taking it with me just in case. As a precaution, like

you said. After all, we don't know who we're dealing with.'

'At least put it back in its sheath . . .' But her words fell on deaf ears.

She stayed put, determined not to let Einar past. In the background she could hear Leó hammering on the door with his fists, kicking it and shouting himself hoarse.

Then her thoughts returned to Anna.

'Einar, you don't think he could have stopped off at Anna's place and hurt her in some way?' she asked, but it was too late: Einar could no longer hear her. He had pushed past and was making for the stairs.

The knife, that lethal blade . . . The world went momentarily black when she thought about what could have happened. Why had Leó lied about seeing no other house on the way to their farm? God, how she wished she could hear the sound of the door opening and Anna's voice calling out to let them know she'd arrived. What if he'd attacked her? The knife had looked clean, but he could have wiped it, of course. A vivid image came into her mind of Anna lying on the ground, helpless, bleeding to death. She was overwhelmed by an overpowering urge to rush out of the front door and down the road to her daughter's house, in defiance of the storm.

'I'm going to find Anna,' she told herself. But hearing the screaming of the wind outside, she knew it would be difficult, if not impossible, to make it there alive.

She went into the sitting room.

'I'm coming in,' she heard Einar saying upstairs in a threatening voice. 'Can you move back from the door?'

The banging stopped and from inside the attic room Erla heard Leó calling: 'Come in, then!'

She was filled with a sick dread about what might happen. The sensible thing would be to race upstairs and force them apart, then order Einar to let the man go. Show Leó the door . . . Or perhaps the door to the cellar under the house. The entrance was outside – let him stay down there. Then they could lock themselves in the house and enjoy their Christmas in peace, putting off the problem until later. They would have to lie to the police. Yes, unfortunately, there was no getting round that. She could do it, though – she was sure she could. She could lie for Einar. Claim indignantly that he'd never locked anyone in. *How ridiculous – my husband would never do anything like that.* Yes, she could probably be pretty convincing if she tried. Because, in spite of everything, she couldn't bear the prospect of life without Einar. Although she would have given almost anything to move away from here, she had long ago resolved to grow old with her husband. The thought of losing him was devastating.

A strange hush had fallen. No doubt Einar was opening the door; yes, she could hear the squeak as the key turned in the lock. Then there was a creaking from the hinges, followed by a barrage of loud, angry questions from her husband: 'What the hell do you want from us? And what's this? Eh, what's this? Why did you come here carrying a weapon?'

Erla couldn't bear to hear any more. Clamping her hands over her ears, she ran for the front door, but had to lower her hands in order to open it, and then she could hear the clash of raised voices from the attic. Whimpering in her desperation, she charged outside, heedless of the fact that she was wearing her indoor clothes, only to discover that it had started snowing again with a vengeance.

She floundered away from the house through the knee-high drifts. The storm had blown up into a blizzard, reducing visibility to no more than a few paces, but she didn't care; she couldn't listen to what was happening inside. Couldn't bear to hear the moment when Einar finally lost control of his temper.

Fervently, pointlessly, she wished that the stranger had never entered their house; that she could turn the clock back twenty-four hours. If she were given another chance, she would slam the door in his face this time.

Another chance . . .

Here she was on Christmas Eve, miles from anywhere. It was a white Christmas – a white Christmas all right, she thought, feeling the urge to laugh hysterically, but there was nothing magical about it. It was shockingly, brutally, cold but she kept going as fast as she could, away from the house, down the slope on what she knew to be the road, although the landmarks were blurred by drifts.

She had the feeling she was running to Anna, although she knew her house was too far off and that she'd never make it there alive, not in this weather, not dressed like this. Yet she felt compelled to flounder on, as if in a nightmare, her body sluggish, pitted against the blizzard, the chill piercing her to the bone, her breath coming in gasps. She wasn't fit enough to keep going at this pace and yet she couldn't stop.

She wasn't going to give in until her body refused to go any further.

The thought flashed through her mind that she could actually die out here, but next moment it was gone and she had returned to obsessing about Einar and his terrible temper; about Anna, her beloved daughter, their only child. And about that stranger who had come to wreck everything; to ruin the life they had spent years, decades, building up for themselves. Maybe she wasn't always happy, not every day, but it was still her life and he had no right – *no right* – to do this. To upset everything.

She slowed to a halt, exhausted, and peering round, her eyes screwed up against the stinging flakes, was shocked to realize how little ground she had covered. All her senses were muffled by the snow. Even though their house wasn't far off, she could make out its shape only in the brief gaps between the curtains of white sweeping across the landscape. It looked drearily dark and inhospitable in the power cut, with no welcoming glow from the windows. Locked in winter's icy grip.

Einar and the visitor were probably still yelling at each other in the attic, and she was glad to be away from the naked show of aggression. Blindly, she blundered forwards again, trying to catch her breath before the wind snatched it away, as if fleeing someone or *something* palpable.

She could feel the suffocating snowflakes filling her nose and mouth, and the cold spreading through her thinly clothed body, but she didn't have time to think about that. Didn't have time to brush the ice from her eyelashes; just kept stumbling on. She knew instinctively that she was following the road. As long as she did that, she couldn't get lost. That absolutely mustn't happen. She was going to turn back, of course, but only after Einar had solved the problem, as he always did. She knew she could count on him.

He could be determined. Stubborn, even angry, but, she kept reminding herself, he had never taken it out on her, let alone on Anna.

Erla was conscious that every step was bringing her closer to Anna's house, although it was still impossibly far away.

She slowed down, unable to keep up the same pace, and halted for a moment, only for the cold to force itself on her consciousness again. Her fingers were numb, and she clenched her fists again and again to get the blood circulating, but it didn't really help. She had to turn back; she couldn't keep up this madness. It was then that she spotted the car.

There it was – their jeep, their old green jeep, hardly recognizable under its thick quilt of snow. Einar always left it parked some distance from the house in winter, since the last slope up to the farm was the most difficult stretch, where the deepest drifts formed.

She snatched a hasty glance over her shoulder, terrified that someone had followed her. Facing into the wind, she squinted against the snow, but couldn't see any sign of pursuit, only a maelstrom of tumbling white flakes.

Erla didn't have the strength to retrace her steps, not without a rest. Her whole body was racked with shivers, her teeth chattering. She started scraping frantically at the snow around the driver's door of the jeep, then wrestled with the handle, her fingers painful with the cold, almost weeping with fear that the mechanism would be frozen. Thank God they never locked it. Finally, she got the door open, dragging it through the soft, piled-up drift until she could crawl in through the gap and get behind the wheel. It was dark in the car, with the windows crusted over with ice. She groped for the ignition, only to find that Einar hadn't left the keys in it, as he usually did, so she wouldn't be able to switch on the engine to get the heater going. Still, although the car was freezing inside, it did at least give her a respite from the storm. She sat there panting, getting her breath back, and closed her eyes for a moment, just to summon her strength, not to fall asleep – she knew she mustn't succumb to the drowsiness that began to steal over her.

XX

Erla woke with a jerk to find herself sitting in the driver's seat of the jeep. She must have dozed off, but had no idea how long for. Given the risk of hypothermia, she was lucky to have woken at all.

Had she heard a noise, or had that been part of her dream?

Stretching her cramped limbs, she peered out of the window to her left, only to come face to face with a pair of eyes staring in at her through a narrow gap that had been cleared in the ice.

She flinched away, breathless with shock, then stiffened with terror. She couldn't see who it was standing out there, looking in at her, but knew she couldn't escape; the jeep wasn't locked and she was as good as trapped in the driver's seat.

In a panic, she dropped her gaze to the door handle, avoiding those horrible eyes, scrabbling frantically to lock the door from inside.

Of course, it would give her just a few seconds' respite,

as she could only reach the driver's door from where she sat. She couldn't get to the other lock without crawling across the wide seat to the passenger side.

A tapping on the glass made her jump and she realized that it must have been this noise that had woken her.

Fighting back her dread, Erla raised her eyes to the window again, her heart pounding, determined this time to get a good look at whoever it was outside. It could only be one of two people: Einar or the visitor. She couldn't let herself start believing in anything supernatural at this stage.

Oh God, she hoped it was Einar.

She strained to see his face through the narrow gap.

It wasn't Einar.

She sat paralysed with fear.

The man tapped on the window again.

'Erla?' she heard him calling, his voice muffled by the glass. He rattled the door handle. 'Erla? Can you open the door? I need to talk to you.'

She tried to answer but her mouth was dry.

'Erla? Please will you come back to the house with me?' This time, she caught the note of fear in his voice. That, in itself, was odd, because if anyone ought to be scared to death, it was her, not him.

Where's Einar? she thought. Why hadn't he come to look for her too? She tried not to let her imagination run away with her. Of course he was all right. Of course. They must have split up and come to search for her separately. Perhaps he had gone to look for her in the barn.

Goodness knows how long she had been gone. Letting

herself fall asleep out here in the car had been a very bad idea indeed. It was still snowing and the rusty old jeep provided little shelter, with the cold air sneaking in through all the gaps in the bodywork.

'Erla, please get out of the car. I need to talk to you!' The man tore at the handle again, and she feared for a moment that the whole door would come off. But however old and rusty it was, it seemed the jeep wasn't about to fall apart.

She looked helplessly around the gloomy interior, then plucked up the courage to meet Leó's eye again. *What do you want from me?* She tried to convey the message wordlessly. Didn't trust herself to speak.

He seemed frightened. Yes, there was no doubt about it. Yet at the same time he terrified her. Both of them scared out of their wits – that was a recipe for disaster. He scraped the window clear so he could see her better and now she took in the fact that he wasn't wearing a coat; like her, he must have charged out into the blizzard without pausing to pull on his outdoor clothes, and his hair and jumper were now plastered with white. He must be freezing too, yet a desperate energy seemed to be driving him on. Erla needed to know what lay behind this, but at the same time she dreaded the truth.

Next minute, he had let go of the handle and was wading as fast as he could round the car. She tried to reach across to the lock on the passenger side but was hampered by being so weak and stiff from the cold.

He got there first and wrenched the door open.

XXI

Never in her life had Erla been so petrified.

She stared at the man, at the intruder who had spoilt their quiet Christmas . . . who had turned up armed with a knife, who had lied to them. No one should have been able to get here at this time of year; they should have been safe, cut off, miles from the nearest settlement.

There was a wild intensity in his eyes, yet for a moment neither he nor Erla moved. Having got the car door open, he didn't seem to know what to do next. Erla shifted almost imperceptibly away from him. He remained quite still, showing no sign of being about to lunge into the car. She began to inch her hand towards the lock on the driver's side, keeping her gaze riveted on Leó all the while.

Then he spoke, his voice hoarse: 'I need to talk to you, Erla. It's urgent.' She didn't say a word, just stared back at him, and after a pause he added something, his words barely audible over the fury of the storm, but she thought it was: 'I'm not going to hurt you, I promise.'

Erla's blood ran cold at the words. Reacting instinctively, she flung open the driver's door and clambered out of the jeep.

Without so much as a backward glance, she set off at a stumbling run, keeping her gaze trained on where the house ought to be. But again, she found herself moving with a dreamlike slowness; the snow was even deeper than it had been earlier and she was almost blinded by the flakes.

At least she intuitively knew where she was going, though, and headed up the familiar slope, as she had countless times before, though never before in such desperate haste, her life depending on it. She was seized by a premonition that something terrible had happened and that she was in real danger, despite the man's assurances to the contrary.

I'm not going to hurt you. She didn't dare look round, didn't want to know how close he was behind her. Didn't dare slow her frantic pace.

As she waded through the drifts, she shrieked into the void as loudly as she could, calling her husband's name, though she knew the sound waves would quickly dissipate among the wildly swirling snowflakes and her despairing cries would be smothered at birth by the gale.

Worse than that, she had a horrible foreboding that there was no one there to hear her call. That something had happened to Einar. She refused to believe it. It couldn't be true.

Where the *hell* was he, though? Why was she alone,

fleeing a dangerous intruder, on Christmas Eve, of all days?

'*Einar!*' Erla would never have believed that she had it in her to screech like that. Terror was clearly a great source of strength.

She was dangerously cold in her thin, indoor clothes, but that didn't matter now. The only thing that mattered was to get into the house before Leó and lock the door behind her. She had to lock him out and make sure all the windows were secured as well. Then she could behave as if nothing had happened, as if it was just a normal day.

A blackness developed at the edges of her vision and began to close in like a tunnel, but she fought against it. She wasn't going to faint; she was so nearly there. She was going to make it, and no one was going to stop her.

She was terrified that any minute now Leó would catch up with her and she would feel his hand grabbing her shoulder, shoving her down in the snow, and . . . and then what? However difficult it was to fight a path back through the drifts to the house, he must surely be able to run faster than her. So why hadn't he caught up already?

She longed to look round and see how much of a head-start she had on him but couldn't bring herself to turn, just kept going.

A dark shape loomed through the whiteness. The house. She was nearly there . . . so very nearly there.

XXII

A carol was playing on the radio in the background, but there was silence at the dinner table.

Hulda had, from habit, laid it with its seasonal finery: a red cloth and plates to match, the best crystal glasses. The malt brew in its crystal jug and the *pièce de résistance*, the gammon, growing colder with every minute that passed.

Hulda and her mother had both helped themselves to food, and the older woman was busy piling her fork with meat, gravy and caramelized potatoes. Hulda hadn't touched hers.

There was no sign of Jón and Dimma.

'He must bring her through soon,' Hulda muttered, staring unseeingly at her plate, more to herself than to her mother.

'Hulda, dear . . .'

Hulda glanced at her mother. After pausing to take another mouthful of ham, the older woman repeated, still chewing: 'Hulda, dear, I don't know how you're bringing her up or how you and Jón usually do things, but it's disgracefully rude of the child not to come to the table for Christmas dinner. I haven't seen her at all yet, and it's Christmas Eve! Behaviour like that would never have been tolerated when I was young – and we'd never have put up with it when you were a girl either.'

'Mum . . .'

Her mother took a swig of malt and orange. 'Shall I go in and try to talk her round? Dimma and I have always been so close.' She smiled a little smugly.

Unlike us, Hulda wanted to retort. But all she said was 'Leave it to Jón,' adding: 'It's all right.' But she didn't believe it herself any more.

'You must both be spending too much time working, Hulda. I'm sure that's what it is. Jón's always flat out and you've got such a demanding job with the police. I just don't think it's right. In my opinion, you ought to pay more attention to the poor child and find yourself an eas-ier way of earning money. Why not get a part-time position, from nine to twelve, or something? After all, I get the impression that Jón brings in more than enough for the whole family.'

'Don't interfere, Mum,' Hulda snapped. Rising from her chair, she called into the hallway: 'Jón, Dimma, are you coming?'

'Well, if you ask me, it's lack of discipline. Sometimes you just have to put your foot down.'

'Put your foot down?'

'Yes, that's what I think.'

'And who do you suggest puts their foot down, hm?' Hulda asked angrily. 'Us? Or you, maybe?'

Her mother was a little flustered by this attack.

'Well . . . don't get me wrong . . . But it's my right as your mother to take an interest in my grandchild's upbringing. I do have a bit of experience with childrearing, after all.'

'Oh, you do, do you? Is that a fact?' Hulda blurted out with sudden venom, only to regret it immediately.

There was a shocked silence. They heard Jón calling: 'Just coming, love.'

'What do you mean by that, Hulda? Just what are you implying?' Her mother sounded near to tears and Hulda sent up an exasperated prayer for patience.

Getting her temper under control, she said quickly: 'I didn't mean anything by it, Mum. Sorry. It just gets on my nerves when you start criticizing us. I know you mean well, but we're having a tricky time with Dimma at the moment and we're doing our best, but it really doesn't help when you interfere.'

This was met by an offended silence and Hulda knew that her mother had heard, behind the innocuous words, an echo of the chasm that had opened up between them over the years; that unbridgeable chasm that Hulda had learned to live with but her mother apparently never had.

Her mother lowered her eyes to her plate and took another mouthful of food.

'You know, Hulda,' she said after she had swallowed, 'that we . . . I tried my best with you . . .' She faltered and her words trailed off, drowned out by the choir on the radio singing 'Silent Night'.

Shortly after this, Jón appeared, frowning heavily, and at first it seemed he wasn't going to say anything at all. He was all too inclined to withdraw into himself and refuse to be sociable in company.

Hulda fixed him with a stare, trying to compel him to tell her what was happening, as it was all too obvious that Dimma wasn't coming out to join them. She thought about the unopened Christmas presents lying under the prettily decorated tree and foresaw a miserable ending to what should have been a happy evening. How she wished her mother would take the hint and leave, but she knew that wasn't going to happen, and they could hardly throw her out, today of all days.

It was her mother who broke the tense silence: 'What's the matter with the child? Shall I go and talk to her?'

Jón hesitated, then sat down at the table.

'Thanks for offering, but it wouldn't do any good.' He poured some malt from the crystal jug into his glass. 'She's not coming out. She doesn't want to.'

'Why not?' Again, it was Hulda's mother who wouldn't let it go.

'I've no idea, I'm afraid. I wish I knew what we could do.' He seemed uncharacteristically despondent. 'It's some kind of obstinacy, some kind of . . . well, teenage rebellion, but on a whole different level. I suppose it's . . . it's . . . the weight of tradition she's rejecting, or something like that – Christmas and all the trappings. I can't explain it.'

'Then you need to shake that nonsense out of her,' Hulda's mother said, rapping the table for emphasis. 'More discipline, that's what's needed.'

'*Mum!*' Hulda shouted. 'Will you just shut up! This has nothing to do with you. Leave it to Jón and me.'

'Well, then, I suppose you'd rather I went home? In the middle of Christmas dinner?' her mother retorted. 'I'll go, if that's what you want, Hulda – if you'd kindly call me a taxi.'

Hulda would have given anything to agree and ring for a cab, but she forced herself to say: 'Of course not! Don't be silly, Mum. Let's just enjoy the food. Try to have a nice evening and open our presents as usual.' She felt a tear running down her cheek. Turning her head away, she wiped it off with the back of her hand and tried to pull herself together.

'Dimma will get over it,' Jón said at last, helping himself to ham.

'She won't get over it, Jón,' Hulda replied sharply, momentarily forgetting her mother's presence. 'She won't get over it. The instant Christmas is over, we need to talk to a doctor or a psychologist or something. I won't listen to any more excuses.'

Embarrassed, Jón glanced first at his mother-in-law, then at Hulda: 'I don't believe that will solve anything, but now's not the moment. We'll discuss it later, love.'

XXIII

Erla grabbed the door handle with both hands. Thank God, it was unlocked, as always, since there had never been anything to fear in this remote, peaceful spot . . .

Opening it, she almost threw herself inside, over the threshold, into the house.

Home and dry.

All she had to do now was lock the door. She could do that by clicking the latch before she closed it. She had to act quickly. But that meant turning round and facing the unseen terror behind her.

She snatched a glance over her shoulder, but Leó was nowhere to be seen.

It took all her willpower to force her numb, white fingers to obey, but after a moment the lock clicked. Then, just as she was about to slam the door shut, she caught sight of him.

He was coming all right – she could make out his shape through the driving sheets of snow – but he was further away than she had expected. This meant she had time to pause for a second look. It was odd, but there was no doubt about it: he was walking, not running. Although he was drawing inexorably closer, he didn't seem to be in any hurry.

The realization overwhelmed her with dread. She slammed the door with all her might, testing it to check it was definitely locked, then heaved a deep sigh of relief, feeling safe at last.

Why the hell wasn't he hurrying?

What did he know that she didn't? That Einar wouldn't be coming to her rescue?

Still panting, she shouted out Einar's name, then caught her breath, trembling with reaction, trying to slow her frantically beating heart and think rationally.

The windows – they were all shut, weren't they? Yes, they must be, in this weather. And anyway, she doubted Leó would be able to squeeze in through any of them, as they were all so small.

The back door?

She dashed through the sitting room and along the dark passage, her arms outstretched to avoid colliding with the walls.

It was locked.

Almost sobbing with relief, she leaned against the wall, briefly closing her eyes. Now that she was safe she became aware of how cold she was, her whole body racked with shivers.

She called out to her husband again. There was no answer.

She took stock of the situation: the phone wasn't

working, there was a power cut, and with every second Leó was drawing closer.

Why couldn't he just disappear? Why couldn't she wake up? Surely this nightmare had to end soon.

It was hard to see anything indoors now that the blizzard had blotted out the last remaining daylight, and she knew from experience that it could take days for the power to be restored. Was she seriously going to have to cower in here for all that time, until Leó had given up and gone? And where, oh, where was Einar?

'Einar!' she shouted again: 'Einar!' so loudly that she knew her call would carry through the whole house, breaking the sinister silence, piercing the darkness. She waited, straining her ears, for a reply.

'Einar!' she shrieked again.

She slid down the wall until she was sitting on the floor at the end of the passage, where the darkness was absolute. There were no windows nearby; here she could sit in a corner, secure in the knowledge that no one could creep up behind her. She felt weak with fatigue.

There was no sound.

Her thoughts flew to Anna again. There was her old room, the door closed as usual. Unlike the attic room, it was never rented out to travellers. Anna's room was left untouched. It had been her private refuge until she went away to boarding school. Later, she had moved back to the countryside, not to her old room, but to the neighbouring farmhouse. Erla had been so glad to have her daughter back, even though it was a bit of a trek between the two houses.

She couldn't see out of any windows from where she was sitting, but she could hear the roaring and whistling of the wind, and sense the storm raging outside, battering the house. Einar had always found weather like this exhilarating and used to remark how cosy it was to listen to the noise of the gale, knowing that they were safe inside, able to watch the elements doing battle from the comfort of home. But then he was a child of nature and belonged to this wild, desolate landscape. She supposed that was the main difference between them.

Where in God's name *was* he? Should she call again? Maybe he couldn't hear her because he had gone to see if she was hiding in the barn.

She couldn't summon the courage to break the silence again. With every passing second, the chances increased that Leó would have given up and gone away, leaving her in peace.

Curse the power cut. How incredibly unlucky could they get? But what else could she expect? It happened far too often in winter, generally during a storm like this one. Of course, they shouldn't put up with it, but they had little influence and repairing the power lines to restore electricity to a couple of scattered farms like theirs was never a priority. Anna's power must be out too; it had to be. She hated the thought of her daughter sitting alone in the dark.

Then there was that business with the phone. That was peculiar. The phone usually worked, whatever happened. Had Einar been right to suspect Leó of tampering with it?

Her shivering subsided a little, but her clothes were

wet and clammy with the melting snow and her paralysing fear showed no sign of shifting.

She sat there in the silent house, trying to block out the noise of the gale outside, listening to hear whether Leó had reached the door and was trying to get in.

Oh God, oh God . . . If he got in, would she be able to spot him in time, in the gathering gloom? She wasn't sure.

Instinct told her to stay pressed into her corner and wait until the whole thing had blown over.

She closed her eyes again, which wasn't the most sensible thing to do in the circumstances, but she simply had to try to concentrate on something else, to get her rising panic under control. She made herself think about Anna and Einar. Imagined that it was Christmas Eve and the three of them were here together: she, Einar and Anna. No one else. And that they had finally opened their presents.

She waited and waited, how long for she didn't know, praying that her wish would come true, but nothing happened.

The urge became too much for her. 'Einar!' she shouted, and listened for his answer. There was no reply but the howling of the wind. 'Einar! Where are you?'

She pushed herself to her feet. It was no good; she would have to search for him, starting indoors. She didn't dare risk going outside, not yet. She wanted to let the storm die down and give Leó time to give up and go away once he'd realized that he was locked out of the house. But her mind kept presenting her with horrifying images. Einar might be lying out there in the snow, injured. And she had been too much of a gutless coward to go and look for him. Maybe . . . But with the weather like this and Leó lying in wait, it would be crazy to venture outdoors. She stood in the corner, paralysed with fear and indecision, until finally, slowly, she took a step forwards.

It was then that she heard the knocking.

The sound seemed to reverberate around the house, drowning out the gusts of wind, as if the storm had suddenly died down, so strong was the effect on her.

Her nightmare was coming true.

Or could she have misheard? It was so hard to tell what was imaginary and what was real.

Though her eyes were growing accustomed to the gloom, she put a hand to the wall to steady herself and felt her way along the passage. She had to get closer to the front door to be able to hear properly. She so desperately wanted it to be Einar out there.

She almost jumped out of her skin when the knocking started up again. A series of heavy blows. To Erla, the message was clear: *You're not safe anywhere.*

She stood quite still, and time seemed to stand still with her.

A succession of foolishly inconsequential thoughts ran through her head. So much for Christmas Eve this year. No *hangikjöt* on the table, no carols on the radio, no presents. And no Christmas books. Usually, the thing she looked forward to most was opening the parcel containing her new novel and reading it late into the night by candlelight. The thought briefly cheered her and she almost, for a moment, managed to forget how remote a dream it was, even though she was in her own home, where she had always been safe, until now.

But nothing could be taken for granted any more, and on some level she knew that, after this, nothing would ever be the same again. The only question now was how this evening, this night, would end.

More heavy thuds on the door. She moved closer to the source, as if in a trance; aware of the danger but unable to stop herself.

She craned her head round the corner into the hall and her heart gave such a sickening lurch that she forgot to breathe when she saw the shadow of a face pressed against the coloured glass of the window beside the front door.

She recoiled so fast she almost fell over backwards.

It was him, that bastard; it was him.

But of course it was him; she already knew that. Who else could it be? And yet she had been hoping, against her better judgement, that it was Einar. That Leó had gone away.

There was no mistaking it, even though the coloured glass blurred his outline; she was certain it was Leó.

'I know you're in there, Erla, I know you are.' At last he spoke – or perhaps she just hadn't been able to hear him until now.

'The door was unlocked before and now you've locked it, so I know you're there!' he shouted. 'Let me in – we need to talk. There's . . . something's happened . . .' He broke off, then resumed: 'I need to know . . .'

No, she thought, *I* need to know – I need to know where Einar is.

But she didn't want to answer. If she did, it would only confirm that she was there, in the house. And for all she knew, he was perfectly capable of breaking the glass panel and reaching in to unlock the door.

He started banging thunderously again, first on the door, then on the window.

Steeling herself, she took a step into the hall, feeling her heart pounding in her chest. She was in uncharted territory. She had to answer. It felt as if she were having an out-of-body experience, as if someone else had taken the decision for her.

'What do you want from me?' she called in a high, thin voice. 'What is it you want? This is *my* house. I don't have to let you in.'

'Are you going to leave me to die of cold out here?'

'It . . . that . . . that has nothing to do with me,' she quavered, feeling her courage ebbing away.

He banged on the door so violently that Erla quailed.

'You have to let me in, Erla.'

'You don't get to tell me what to do.'

There was silence.

'Where's Einar?' she called.

No reply.

'I'll open the door if you tell me where Einar is,' she said at last, though she had no intention of keeping her side of the bargain. For all she cared, the bastard could freeze to death on the doorstep. She wasn't letting him anywhere near her.

The answer was so long in coming that she started to wonder if he was still out there. She felt a crazy hope that he'd gone, she didn't care where. Gone, never to return. Or that he had been nothing but a figment of her imagination all along . . .

As if the situation wasn't bad enough already, the darkness had really got her spooked. Normally, power cuts didn't have this effect on her, but now she couldn't bear it; she would have to find a candle. Yes, that was it . . . There were candles on the dining table. But even as she turned, she heard his voice again.

'I'll tell you where he is if you open the door.'

A prickle of fear ran down her spine.

She tried to work out what this meant. Did he know where Einar was? Or was he lying? Had he done something to him – locked him in somewhere, perhaps? Or was Einar still outside looking for her, in the cold and snow?

Facts and conjecture spun in her head until she felt dizzy, no longer sure what was true, disorientated in the gloom, terrified of the man standing outside the door, of the sudden lull, the calm before the storm . . .

Then her head cleared a little. She began inching her way towards the sitting room, acting as if Leó wasn't there. She had to get a grip on the situation. Of course he wasn't going anywhere. Sooner or later, he would break into the house. There was no one to help her; she would have to fend for herself.

Feeling the edge of the dining table, she fumbled over the surface until she found a candle. Matches. Where were the matches? Generally, Einar kept some in his pocket, a habit from back when he used to smoke. But he wasn't here. And, anyway, he'd given the box to Leó, hadn't he? She remembered now.

She had to think fast. There was no sound from Leó at the moment and again this fact sent a stab of cold fear through her. Think, she told herself. Both the doors were definitely locked, which meant he couldn't get in without making a noise.

Wait a minute – hadn't she seen a box of matches in the kitchen? Above the fridge? She made her way in there, reached up to the shelf and groped along it. For a moment she was afraid she'd been wrong. But no, there was the box. Hurriedly, she pulled out a match and tried to strike it, but her hands were shaking so badly that it wouldn't light.

Erla tried again, the match rasped and flared, and she raised the small, bright flame carefully, trying to steady her hand, to the candle. Light, at last.

The sight stirred up a fleeting memory of the old days, when Anna was small and the electricity supply had been even more capricious. Family evenings by candlelight had seemed delightful then. More often than not, the three of them had sat down to play cards together – whist had been a favourite – but Einar hadn't always been in the mood, so mother and daughter used to play together by the soft radiance. That's what Anna's childhood had been like, a perpetual struggle with the elements, but then she had gone away to school and Erla had clung to the hope that Anna would break free from the fetters of the past. The relentless hard graft had to end with her and Einar. Erla was determined that their daughter should settle in a town, where life would be that bit easier. But then Anna had announced, out of the blue, that she was moving home to the countryside, still single, still far too young, to take over the neighbouring tenant farm, which also belonged to them. No one had dreamt that anyone would ever move back here, but Anna had wanted to renovate the house and land to prevent it from falling into decay. The house had been a favourite haunt when she was a child and she'd made up her mind that this was where she wanted to live. She would worry about finding a husband and starting a family later. 'It'll happen when it happens,' she had said.

Erla remembered that conversation so well. It was the first time she had ever truly lost her temper with her daughter. She had berated her for her decision to move back home, and been furious with herself for never having said anything to Einar, never having suggested in all seriousness that they should move. Anna's response had left her stunned. It had come home to her then that her daughter really wanted to live there, that she genuinely loved the district, the moors, the sheep, the weather, all of it. Just like Einar. A chip off the old block . . . Whereas she herself couldn't be more different from her daughter. She had never raised the subject with Anna again.

Erla snapped out of her thoughts to find herself still standing there in the kitchen, her eyes dwelling on the flickering flame. Leó had started banging on the door again. He obviously wasn't going to give up, but it seemed he wasn't about to break in – not yet, anyway. And she had no intention of ever letting him in herself.

At least she could see her surroundings now. She held up the candle, looking around the kitchen, then went into the sitting room. There was nobody there. Of course there wasn't; she would have noticed if there had been. And nothing appeared to have been disturbed either; everything was in its place, where it ought to be . . . But no, that wasn't true. *They should have been sitting at the dinner table*, the family, eating smoked lamb. *That's* how it should have been.

Where on earth was Einar? Could he be up in the attic? Could he be lying there injured from a fight with Leó? She went cold at the thought.

She was aware of the relentless hammering on the door in the background, but ignored it. All she could think about was going upstairs and finding out if Einar was there. But her legs felt heavy and her fear was growing with every minute.

One step at a time, with a terrible, dragging reluctance, she climbed the stairs; the racket Leó was making reached her like an echo from another world.

She was more conscious now of her own heartbeat booming in her ears than of any external noises.

As soon as she made it up on to the landing, she saw that the door to the guestroom was open. Immediately, instinct warned her that something dreadful had happened there and her first impulse was to run away, downstairs, out of the house – anything to avoid having to face up to the truth.

She stood stock still, aware that time was running out. If Leó had hurt Einar in some way, she had to know. She needed time to react and work out an escape plan.

She took the last few steps to the doorway, keeping her head down, not daring to look into the room, not quite yet. Then she held the candle aloft so it would illuminate the whole space, closed her eyes, feeling herself break out in a sweat, and opened them again.

The shock was so horrible that for a moment she couldn't move, couldn't think. Then, from deep within her subconscious, a thought broke through to the surface: freedom.

She was free at last.

At long last she could leave this place, throw off the crushing weight of her loneliness, move to a larger community, meet people, make friends, see more of her family; no longer be a prisoner in her own home for months on end . . .

Then the sickness and the shame took over and she was appalled by her involuntary reaction.

There on the floor lay her husband, the love of her life, deathly still, surrounded by a dark, spreading stain.

XXIV

Erla tried to scream, but her throat wouldn't produce any sound. Afraid she was going to throw up, she crouched down and drew a deep, shuddering breath, closing her eyes, trying to steady herself. Maybe she was seeing things; maybe there was nothing there: no body, no blood. She forced herself to look up, only to start retching again at the sight.

Next moment the fear took over as the reality sank in that she was alone, *alone*, and that Leó must have murdered Einar — there could be no other explanation.

The man who was standing outside the house, demanding to be let in, was a cold-blooded killer.

Her life was in danger. It must be. She had a sudden mad impulse to break out through the dormer window but knew it wouldn't work. The window was small, the roof steep, and she was bound to be swept off by the wind. Besides, *he* was out there. She had to think fast if she was going to get out of this alive. Feeling a wet splash on her hand, she realized she was crying.

There was no time to mourn Einar now – that would have to wait. She had to save her own life first. But the flow of tears wouldn't be stemmed.

She pressed her fingers to the neck of the motionless body to make quite sure that Einar was no longer breathing. No, there was no question: he was dead. The blood had told her as much, but it had been her last hope. Of course, it was futile anyway, because even if he had still been showing faint signs of life, help was impossibly far away and they were completely cut off from the outside world.

Erla straightened up and hurried out of the room and down the stairs, clutching the candlestick, not wanting to risk being plunged into darkness again. It could only be a matter of time before Leó broke his way in. She wondered why he hadn't already done so. Did he want to win her trust, to save himself a struggle? He had already killed a man, so there was no reason to believe he would spare her.

Yet fear had given her a sudden burst of adrenaline and she walked towards the front door with a sure tread. There was no sound from outside, but she had to know if he was still there: 'What do you want from me?' she called, her voice hard and unwavering now.

There was no answer at first, which she found unnerving, then eventually Leó replied, his teeth audibly chattering: 'Please let me in. Please. It's so cold out here – it's still snowing – and I need to talk to you.'

'About what?'

'You know what, Erla. You know.'

Her heart missed a beat and for a moment the walls seemed to be closing in on her. She had a vision that the snow had vanished, it was autumn, and a chill crept up on her, sending a shiver through her body. She shook herself.

'What do you want from me?' she repeated at last.

Before he could answer, she was away, running out of the hall, taking care not to make any noise, determined to fool Leó into thinking that she hadn't moved. She put the candle down on the coffee table, snuffed it out, then ran along the passage to the kitchen to fetch the spare keys that were hanging from the hook on the wall. She knew just where to lay her hands on them in the dark. Then she hared back through the sitting room, past the stairs, past the bedrooms, to the back door, where she had sat earlier, wishing she could wake up from this nightmare.

Her mind was working furiously. There was no point trying to escape on foot and make her way to Anna's house or the village beyond it, not in these conditions. He would easily catch up with her, and the poor old jeep, valiant as it was, wouldn't be able to make any headway through the deep drifts blocking the road.

She opened the back door with infinite care, half expecting Leó to materialize outside, having guessed that she might be planning to escape that way; terrified that she would run slap into him. She was breathing in shallow gasps but, to her immense relief, she couldn't see any sign of him near the house. Instead, she was knocked sideways by a violent gust that swept a wave of freezing snow over her and into the house. The ferocity of the storm was incredible. No wonder the electricity had gone. In weather like this, something had to give.

She closed the door noiselessly behind her, making sure that the lock clicked.

No turning back now.

Erla peered round the corner, screwing up her eyes against the blizzard, hardly able to see a thing but almost sure that Leó was nowhere near. He must still be at the front door, pleading with her to let him in, talking to her in the belief that she was listening just inside. She made a wild dash for the steps that led down to the cellar under the house. She could wait it out there. There were no windows, the door was thick and strong, and there were all kinds of tools and other implements that she could use in self-defence, if it came to that, and – most importantly of all – there was a supply of tins and perishable foods like potatoes.

She picked her way gingerly down the steps to the cellar door. The last thing she wanted was to slip and injure herself now. She tried to close her mind to the images that flashed into it.

Then she had to find the right key by feel; clumsy, fumbling in the dark, ready to cry with frustration. She snatched another look round before turning the key in the lock but, thank God, there was no one behind her.

As usual, it required a bit of a shove to open the door. Only when it gave way, scraping back into pitch blackness, did she realize that in her hysterical flight she had forgotten to bring any candles or matches.

Hell.

She tried to weigh up the alternatives, aware that there was no time to lose. Either waste precious minutes going back into the house or wait down here in the darkness. Neither alternative was good. Desperately, she tried to think straight. She couldn't rely on Leó to remain unsuspecting by the front door much longer. Any minute now, he was going to come hunting for another way in. No, it wasn't worth the risk. Heaving a deep breath, she stepped inside the cellar and forced the door shut behind her.

XXV

This new predicament was like nothing Erla had ever experienced before. She stood there, clinging on to the door handle as if it was a lifeline, not daring to move, utterly blind in the pitch-black cellar.

Of course, she had known it would be dark, but it was one thing to know something, another to experience it first hand. She was afraid of becoming disorientated the moment she let go of the handle. As long as she held on to it, she could at least be confident of the way out.

As a child, Erla had been afraid of the dark, but as an adult she'd thought she'd got over it. Now, though, the unreasoning terror quickened inside her again, the fear of what was lurking in the shadows. For a moment, she even had the crazy idea that Leó might be down there too; that he'd got hold of a key somehow and was lying in wait for her. She began to whimper.

Next minute, common sense kicked in. There was no way he could be down here. That was impossible. He would have had to move incredibly fast to get here before her, and there had been no footprints in the snow on the steps – unless there had been and she had failed to notice them? She forced herself to take deep breaths and push these foolish thoughts away. Of course she was alone down there. She mustn't let herself get hysterical.

Gradually, she noticed how dry and stale the air was in the windowless, enclosed space and wondered if this had been a terrible mistake. The spectre of claustrophobia began to raise its head. Erla had always had to train her mind not to dwell on the feeling of being trapped in winter when the farm was snowed in, but now the feeling of panic rose up to clutch at her throat. It was freezing down here too. She wouldn't be able to survive long in this temperature, however much tinned food there was.

Her fingers were numb and cramped from hanging on to the door handle in an attempt to master her fear. As long as she knew where the door was, she reassured herself, she could get out again any time she wanted to. What terrified her almost more than anything else was the thought of getting confused and lost in the lightless cellar.

But these fears were foolish, she reminded herself, as long as Leó was still out there, hunting for her. He was the real threat. She must hold on to that thought. What would she do if he knocked on this door? If he tried to break in? She wondered how long she was prepared to wait down there. Until he left, she supposed. But where was he supposed to go? He was a prisoner of the snow too, no more able to leave than she was.

The more she thought about it, the more inevitable the outcome seemed: sooner or later she would have to face a reckoning with Leó.

But she was going to do everything in her power to avoid it.

XXVI

Erla was sitting in a huddle now, her back pressed against the door, arms hugging her knees in a futile attempt to keep warm as she stared unseeingly into the blackness. She was losing track of how long she had been down there. It was as if time itself had got lost in the dark.

She couldn't hear the wind any more. Perhaps the storm was subsiding. All she knew was that she was safe for now. She was alone down here, Leó was nowhere near and he didn't know where she was. Unless, of course, he saw her footprints leading from the back door to the cellar steps, but hopefully they would have been blurred over by the blowing snow.

When she had made the snap decision to take refuge in the cellar, she'd been thinking of the cans of food stored down there, but now she'd realized that she hadn't even thought to bring a tin opener with her. So much for a long-term solution. Sooner or later she would have to go outside and confront not only Leó but her husband's death; the knowledge that he was lying in a pool of his own blood in the attic.

The thought came to her like a vague echo of something disturbing, horrifying. But she felt bizarrely detached. It seemed so unreal. Her mind couldn't comprehend it.

Had Leó killed Einar?

Had she really seen his body?

She remembered their first meeting so well. She had been nineteen, no more than a child, but her future had been decided then and there. He had been so handsome — he still was, to be fair, though in a different way. A charmingly innocent, mild-mannered country boy in the city. She had fallen head over heels for him that first night, at the dance at Reykjavík's famous Hótel Borg. They had spent all evening dancing with each other, while he told her about life in the countryside, painting a beguiling picture of the moors and mountains, the birds and sheep, and in those days she'd still had a romantic streak, though that had disappeared long ago. Even at twenty he had talked seriously about the importance of keeping the remote farm going, about his sense of duty to the land. She had listened, entranced, and at once started imagining what it would be like to live out there.

It seemed strange to remember how enthusiastic she had been about the idea of moving to the countryside. She supposed it had been partly from a youthful desire to rebel, to do something that would shock her parents.

They had objected all right. It wasn't that they had disapproved of Einar; that would have been unthinkable since he had been such a likeable young man. They'd been impressed by his good manners, and he had come across as well read too. Her parents had certainly appreciated that. But they had kept harping on at them both, repeatedly asking Einar if he wouldn't like to see what it was like to live in the city for a change. Try something different. Erla had known from the first moment, though, that his mind was made up, and she herself had made no attempt to persuade him to change it. Ironic though it seemed now, she had actually been eager to move to the farm.

Since then she had developed a love–hate relationship with this place. However desperate she was to get away, she couldn't leave Einar and Anna behind. They were all held together by such unbreakable bonds. And she could feel the tug of this lonely spot too; without wanting to, she had put down roots in the soil here. Some things couldn't be changed. Perhaps the truth was that she would never get away. In fact, she had long ago become resigned to the fact, even as she suffered torments from the solitude.

This was their home; hers, Einar's and Anna's. The family belonged here. There was no getting past that fact.

She had closed her eyes. That way she could shut out the darkness and let the scenes play out vividly in her mind.

Her thoughts drifted. The mist had descended again, making it so hard to distinguish what was real from what was imaginary. God, she hated the winter. Why did a blizzard have to blow up on Christmas Eve, of all days? Anna must be stuck at home. Unless Leó had harmed her somehow? The thought was so unbearable that Erla did her best to push it away. She had to make herself believe that Anna was safe and sound at home. It was sad to think of her there all alone, but she had always been so independent and self-contained, like her father. Erla hoped she'd at least treat herself to a good meal. A storm like this could last several days before it blew itself out.

Erla would just have to hang on until Anna could get through to the farm. The smoked lamb could wait. It would keep.

She had definitely bought Anna's present, hadn't she? And wrapped it up? Einar's present was in the sitting room, she was sure of that. His book. And then there was her customary novel, her gift from Einar, of course; she couldn't wait to get her hands on that.

If only she had a book to read now – and a little light of course – things wouldn't seem quite so bleak. She didn't need anything else, just to escape for a while, steal away from grim reality into a fictional world. Tomorrow was the twenty-fifth. She would have time to read then, though naturally she would steal a peek at her book tonight, as she always did.

She was so terribly cold. She couldn't stop shivering, couldn't stop her clenched teeth rattling. It was foolish to sit still like this. She should be pacing about to keep warm. And yet she stayed put, too afraid to relinquish her contact with the door, the one fixed point in the lightless world. She kept her eyes tight shut, but the silence was menacing. She had to focus on something positive. Again, she guided her thoughts back to those early years with Einar. She had been captivated the first time she set eyes on this place, thinking to herself: *I want to live here for the rest of my life.*

His parents had welcomed her with open arms. And she had felt at home with them right away, accepted as one of the family, taking part in all the chores, learning about the farm, the animals, enjoying the closeness to nature. Then winter had set in, that first winter, and she'd had a taste of the suffocating claustrophobia that would later come to dominate her existence, though she had tried to ignore it. She'd learned to distract herself by keeping busy, retreating into books and taking refuge with Einar, who knew the land, knew the weather, knew how to comfort her and reassure her that everything would be fine. He had always looked after her, all these years — decades now. Of course, she could never leave him, never abandon him to his fate.

Then, the following year, Anna had come along. Although it hadn't been the plan to have children straight away, it had been a nice surprise and the little girl had immediately become the focus of her parents' and grandparents' existence. To begin with, Erla had pictured them always living there, but later she had grown increasingly determined to get Anna away, help her set up somewhere else. Though in that, alas, she had failed.

Erla could feel herself becoming drowsy but knew she mustn't fall asleep, not here in the freezing cold. She might never wake up again. Had she been dozing? She was confused and opened her eyes, but there was no change, just another, much worse, almost tangible darkness. This wouldn't do. She couldn't feel her fingers or toes. She rose stiffly to her feet, deciding she must walk around the cellar to get her circulation going and prevent her thoughts from wandering but, above all, to keep herself awake. She took a few wary steps, keeping a hand on the wall, not daring to venture too far from the door.

She had the feeling that she was waiting for Einar. But she didn't know why. Could he really have told her to wait down there? In the dark cellar?

She took a few more tentative steps and next minute something soft brushed against her face and she screamed, raising her hands to fight it off, feeling something moving, swinging against her. For an instant she was sure it was alive and screamed again, only to realize a moment later that it must be the brace of ptarmigan Einar had shot last week and hung down here in the cellar. But by then she was no longer sure where the door was, couldn't feel the wall any more, was completely disorientated, couldn't tell how long she'd been down there, couldn't breathe. She was lost in the dark, shut in, a prisoner . . . She stood still for a moment, fighting the rising hysteria, then started moving again, too fast, only to bash her head against some unseen object. The pain was agonizing. She clasped her hands over her skull and felt, or thought she felt, blood oozing from the wound. Damn it.

She squatted down on the floor, closing her eyes again, emitting a low moaning. The world began to spin. She couldn't catch hold of her thoughts. What in God's name was she doing in here?

Where was Einar?

Why hadn't he come?

And where was Anna?

Erla struggled to think what to do. Should she go out

and search for her husband? He must be up in the house, in the sitting room. Or in the barn, perhaps. Maybe it was feeding time. Did he know she was in the cellar? Had she somehow locked herself in or could she get out if she wanted to? She was feeling so muddled that she wondered vaguely if she might be concussed.

Better to stay where she was for now. Keep her eyes closed, take deep, slow breaths and imagine that she was somewhere else.

But one thing she was sure of: it was Christmas Eve.

Then she heard music. Or thought she did. Yes, surely it was the carol service? The church choir singing the Christmas service on the radio. The sweet notes of 'Silent Night' – she could hear them loud and clear.

When she opened her eyes, the music was abruptly cut off and the darkness, the screaming darkness, closed in on her. The world started spinning again and she felt sick. She was losing her grip, losing her balance, suffocating in the airless cellar.

Oh God, where's Einar? she thought. He must be coming soon, to open the door and let her out into the fresh air.

There's nothing to be afraid of.

She waited for a while, shivering, crouching there in this strange, lightless limbo. She didn't know how long for. Then she stood up, cautiously, to avoid banging her head again, her breathing coming in fast, shallow gasps, her mind filled with a single thought: she had to get out. She started moving fast, blundering, confused, then slowed down, but still managed to crash into something. She was lost in a rectangular labyrinth.

She held out her arms in front of her, feeling for the way out. What was that? A shelf. And that was some kind of tool, yes. Concentrate. That meant the door must be on the other side. She had to get out, had to get some air, whatever happened. She felt her way cautiously along the wall, knowing that this way she would find the door in the end.

Erla wished the music would come back. She couldn't understand how she could have heard the carol so clearly, couldn't understand anything any more. All she knew was that she had to get out. 'Silent Night' was such a beautiful carol; it had always been a great favourite of hers. She stood still, closed her eyes, and there it was again, the singing. She smiled, though she couldn't really work out what was happening. Surely the service had finished hours ago? It must be night by now.

How she longed for tomorrow morning. After this horrible experience, she was going to take it easy, put her feet up and read the books that were still lying unopened under the tree. There was the lamb too, they still had that, and some malt brew to drink and a whole box of chocolates. She smiled again at the thought and felt herself growing calmer. After a moment, she started moving slowly, tentatively, her numb fingertips brushing the wall, knowing that any minute she would feel the door.

Then a man's voice called out: 'Are you in there?' The words smashed into her thoughts, shockingly loud and real, followed by a rattle, as someone took hold of the door handle. Someone wanted to get in, but now she remembered that she had locked the door from the inside.

Einar. He'd come for her at last.

She took a couple more steps, felt wood under her fingertips, gripped the handle and turned the key.

She opened the door.

XXVII

Christmas Day.

This was normally one of Hulda's favourite days of the year. After all the stress of getting the house clean and dinner ready on Christmas Eve, the twenty-fifth was a day of relaxation, which she liked to spend quietly absorbed in the books she'd been given, especially since Dimma had grown old enough to entertain herself. Even Jón generally took a break from work and lounged in front of the TV or read the papers.

The twenty-fifth was sacred; they never left the house and avoided all social contact – not that they received many invitations. Jón was an only child. His parents, who'd had him late, were no longer alive and he didn't have many relatives. So there were just the three of them in their little family. They had always looked out for one another, and Hulda had felt it was her role to look after Jón and Dimma. But this year nothing was as it should be and she was at a loss to know why. It was as if the family was disintegrating, as if Dimma was tearing her and Jón apart. Of course, the world doesn't stand still, she knew that; things change. But these were no ordinary changes. There was no obvious explanation for Dimma's strange withdrawal.

Hulda was almost counting down the minutes until the holiday was over and she could call a psychologist. There must be some sort of emergency service available, but following her conversation with Jón she had decided not to look into it. No, the family would just have to paper over the cracks until Christmas had run its course.

It didn't help that Hulda was on duty today. Rare though it was for anything serious to happen on the twenty-fifth, someone still had to be available in CID. But she couldn't keep her mind on the job. Her thoughts were entirely preoccupied with the problem of Dimma. She hadn't seen her daughter for nearly twenty-four hours. The girl hadn't come out of her room at all on Christmas Eve except to go to the bathroom, in spite of all their attempts to put pressure on her to join them at the table. Hulda wasn't worried about her being hungry as Jón had taken a tray of food up to her room. Besides, Dimma was perfectly cap-able of feeding herself, sneaking out to fetch something from the fridge when no one else was around. Teenagers were constantly hungry.

Hulda didn't usually slope off home at midday, but this time she was going to make an exception. Her shift was supposed to last all day, but she'd take a good long lunch break and just hope that nothing would come up at the police station while she was away. If the worst came to the worst, they could always call her at home. She hadn't achieved a single thing that morning anyway. The office was almost empty, and a bit creepy on this loneliest shift of the year.

Hulda hadn't forgotten that she owed the couple in Gardabær a phone call, but she didn't like to ring them on Christmas morning. She was guessing that all they wanted was the same as they had for weeks now: to ask for news of the investigation. But, unfortunately, there was nothing to tell and the odds were vanishingly small that their daughter would be found alive after all this time. Then again, perhaps she had deliberately run away, out of a desire to make a break with her parents. It had emerged during the inquiry that she had decided to take a year off between school and university to travel around Iceland and that her parents had heard from her only intermittently since she'd left. It was conceivable that something had been going on under the surface at home which no one wanted to admit. And, of course, travelling alone around the country was inherently risky. It wasn't impossible that the girl had gone out hiking or even climbing in the highlands on her own. Iceland could be an inhospitable, hazardous environment at any time of year, as an experienced hiker like Hulda was well aware. Yet, in spite of the dangers, she had always felt most at peace with herself in the wild interior.

She got out the case files yet again, since she had nothing better to do, and sat looking at the photo of the girl. She was beautiful, with long red hair and haunting eyes. Hulda had sometimes wondered – against her better judgement, of course – whether she could read any clue in that unfathomable gaze. This was a girl who had gone on a voyage of self-discovery, far from friends and family, only to vanish without trace.

Then suddenly it was Dimma's gaze she was seeing. It used to be so bright and innocent, but since she'd entered her teens, her blue eyes had been shadowed with sadness.

Hulda was too distracted to concentrate. Her thoughts kept returning to the situation at home, feeling Dimma's pain, unable to understand how Jón could be so calm about things. She knew he was intending to have a lie-in for once, so she had promised herself not to ring too early. But it was nearly eleven and there was no reason to think he'd still be asleep. It wasn't a luxury he usually allowed himself, workaholic that he was. She picked up the receiver to call, then, abruptly changing her mind, rose to her feet. She would take her lunch break early instead.

There was a nip in the air outside, but the snow that had fallen on St Thorlákur's Mass had been washed away and the ground was bare, making it feel autumnal rather than wintry. This was just as well since there were few ploughs out on high days and holidays, and reliable though her Skoda was, she didn't trust it in heavy snow. Usually, Hulda hated snowless Christmases, finding them dark and dreary without the white backdrop to reflect the fleeting winter daylight, but today she had no thoughts for anything but her daughter.

Her drive was the same, day in, day out, the ten or so kilometres from the police station in Kópavogur to their house on the Álftanes peninsula, but today she drove like an automaton, totally unaware of her surroundings. All her thoughts were concentrated on the problems at home. As she approached their dear old house, with the sea stretching out flat and grey beyond it, she realized that of course she should never have gone to work. She should have called in sick. After all, it was true that she was in no state to be on duty. As she thought this, she was overwhelmed by a wave of unease so powerful that it almost frightened her.

She parked the car in front of the garage and walked quickly to the house, obeying a sudden, inexplicable need to hurry. She was almost panting in her haste to get inside and see Jón and Dimma. This time she wasn't going to put up with any nonsense: Dimma would have to come out of her room and talk to them – her behaviour was totally unacceptable. Hulda was determined to make a last-ditch attempt to get their family life back on track. She rang the bell but there was no answer, then knocked, but nothing happened. She started rummaging in her coat pocket for the bunch of keys, but it took her longer than usual to find them. She was all fingers and thumbs once she finally got them out and tried to insert the front door key into the lock. At last she succeeded and burst into the house, only to come face to face with Jón, who was standing awkwardly in the hall.

'Sorry, I fell asleep again. That's why it took me so long to come to the door. I must have been out like a light. I woke when you left this morning, then went back to bed with a book. Don't know what came over me; I don't usually sleep that long.' He smiled, blinking blearily. 'I must just be knackered after the last few months – all that backbreaking work and now the problems with Dimma.'

'You need to be careful, Jón. You've got to look after your heart. Remember what the doctor said. You are taking your pills, aren't you?'

'Of course. I'm not taking any risks.'

'And . . . and . . .' She braced herself for the answer she dreaded. 'Is Dimma awake? Has she come out of her room?'

Jón shook his head. 'No, as far as I know, she's still asleep.'

'Haven't you tried to wake her?'

He hesitated. 'No, I haven't had a chance. Besides, it's a holiday. And our attempts to talk to her yesterday evening weren't exactly a success. She just needs some time, poor kid.'

Hulda came further inside without bothering to take off her shoes and coat. 'No, this has gone far enough, Jón.'

'What do you mean?'

'I mean exactly what I say. You can't excuse behaviour like this day after day, right through Christmas, by dismissing it as just a phase she's going through. Or that all teenagers are like that. Look, I know Dimma's our only child, the only teenager we've ever had to deal with, but no way can you expect me to believe that this is normal. It can't possibly be normal.'

'Calm down, love. We'll sort it out together.' He blocked her way, then turned and walked resolutely in the direction of Dimma's room. He knocked, politely at first. 'Let's just see, love. I'll talk to her. I'll take care of this.'

Then he added, as if it had only just dawned on him: 'Why aren't you at work?'

'I can't work with this going on, Jón. And *we*'ll take care of this together. I'm not letting you shoulder all the responsibility.'

There was no answer from inside the room.

Jón rapped again, a little louder than before.

'Dimma!' he called. 'Let us in. Your mum's home from work.'

'Dimma, darling,' Hulda interrupted, 'open the door for us. I need to talk to you. We have to talk.'

There was still no response. But in her imagination Hulda could hear Dimma saying: *We needed to talk a long time ago. Why only now, Mum? Why not before?*

The same sense of unease took hold of her, even more powerfully than before, and for the first time Hulda was properly frightened.

She pushed Jón out of the way. 'Open the door, Dimma! Open up!' She started pounding with both fists on the flimsy old door that was keeping them apart from their daughter, half expecting Jón to try and stop her, to tell her to take it easy, to wait and see, but he hung back. Perhaps he had finally accepted that the situation was serious.

'Open up!' Hulda banged harder than before, her knuckles aching. It occurred to her that Dimma might have slipped out in the night and gone . . . gone where? Her door was locked from the inside and there was no way of climbing out of her window, as it didn't open far enough. No, she was in there, she had to be, so why wasn't she answering?

Before Hulda knew what she was doing, she had started violently kicking the door.

'Hulda, let's . . .' Jón gently caught hold of her arm.

'We're going to get into our daughter's room,' she said in a voice that brooked no opposition, and kicked the door again, as hard as she could.

'Dimma, please open up!' Jón shouted.

Then he shoved Hulda aside and pushed his shoulder against the door with all his strength. When nothing happened, he took a few steps back and ran at it. It didn't give but came close.

He rammed it again and this time there was a loud crack and the door flew wide open.

Hulda couldn't see inside because Jón was blocking her view, but then she dodged round him and looked in.

The sight that met her eyes was so unspeakably, so unimaginably horrific that it robbed her of almost every last ounce of strength. With all that was left to her, she screamed at the top of her voice.

Two months later – February 1988

I

The days following Hulda and Jón's discovery of Dimma's body were lost in a haze.

Hulda could remember the moment when Jón broke the door open, but almost immediately afterwards a sort of amnesia had descended, blotting out the subsequent events. The trauma had proved too much even for a tough policewoman like her, although she had experienced her share of grim sights during her years on the force.

She had been wandering around in a stupor ever since. But even that hadn't prevented her from finally seeing things in their true light. When she looked back at the events leading up to her daughter's death, she realized just how blind she had been. The resulting mental torture was beyond anything she had ever known. Her mind was racked one minute with self-accusations, the next with violent hatred towards Jón. As the numbness began to recede, she couldn't bear to be at home. She had to get out, go to work – do something, anything, to disperse her thoughts and give her a temporary respite from this hell on earth.

And now, here she was, having just landed in the small town of Egilsstadir, the largest community in the east of Iceland, accompanied by two forensic technicians whose job it was to carry out the crime-scene investigation. The journey east had brought no improvement in the weather, especially not here, so far inland. Snow lay deep on the ground and pewter-coloured clouds hung low over the open landscape, almost brushing the tops of the distant fells. The milky waters of the long, narrow lake were grey and bleak under the wintry sky, the stands of dark pine forest along its shores making the scene appear strangely un-Icelandic.

They were met at the airport by a middle-aged representative of the local force called Jens, who had come to pick them up in a big police four-by-four. Hulda would have preferred to take the wheel herself, as she hated being driven by other people, but she could hardly ask this man, who turned out to be an inspector, to move over into the passenger seat for her.

Even in the off-roader, the journey turned out to be far from easy. Away from the lake, the landscape was harsh and treeless. The roads were treacherously icy and the snow grew deeper the further they travelled from the town, making progress achingly slow. They were driving through what seemed an interminably long, empty, U-shaped valley between rugged hills when the inspector broke the silence.

'Not far now to the farm,' he remarked. 'The road's

been more or less impassable since Christmas. No one had seen or heard from the couple – Einar and Erla, that is – for a couple of months and they couldn't be reached by phone either, so I decided to check up on them. See how the winter had treated them, you know. And . . . well . . .'

He had no need to say any more: Hulda had been shown the photographs from the crime scene. She had spent most of the journey worrying about whether she was in any fit state to cope with this case. Worse, she could sense that her colleagues also had their doubts about her state of mind. When they'd stopped at a petrol station earlier to buy hot-dogs and Coke, she had noticed her two companions from Forensics conferring in low voices and could tell from their expressions that they were talking about her. Goodness knows, it was understandable.

Mostly, she was aware of their sympathy, but even that made her uncomfortable. She felt as if her colleagues had discovered her weak spot, and the thought was unbearable. She hated the idea of letting her guard down for fear they would think of her as an emotional woman who wasn't tough enough for the job. But none of this really mattered; it was rendered utterly trivial by what had happened at Christmas. Then another voice in her head kicked in, telling her that if she didn't pick herself up again soon, she never would.

She would have to do it alone. Although she and Jón were still living under the same roof, in her eyes he might as well be dead.

There had been an awkward silence in the car for much of the way. Hulda was sure it was because her companions didn't know how to act around her after what had happened. Their behaviour got on her nerves. Surely it should be up to her to decide when she was ready to come back to work? Anyway, like it or not, she was here. If taking on the case had been a mistake, that was her business. She couldn't stand having people tiptoeing around her, even though it was entirely well meant. She couldn't stand being a victim.

It had begun to snow, quite heavily, the thick flakes clogging the windscreen wipers. 'It'll be fine,' the inspector said, reading her mind. He was about ten years older than her, overweight, with a deep voice and thin, wispy hair. 'We're used to it here. A bit of snow doesn't bother us – this is nothing compared to what it was like up here at Christmas.'

He got no response from the back seat, where the two Forensics guys were sitting, so it was up to Hulda to reply, rather curtly: 'Right.'

Inspector Jens took this as an invitation to carry on talking: 'It looks to me like some kind of tragic domestic. Of course, I wouldn't want to jump to conclusions, but I don't see how it could have been anything else. Anyway, I sent two strong lads to the scene after I found the bodies, to secure the place until you could get here. They're still up there in the cold, poor boys. I hope they'll have the sense to wait indoors.' He seemed unable to stop talking now that he had started. 'I just don't understand how the couple could have clung on up there for so long. Of course, it was Einar's family home, but it was the only farm left in the whole valley. All the other inhabitants gave up trying to scrape a living out here and upped sticks a long time ago.'

'Right,' Hulda repeated shortly, hoping this would deter him from continuing.

'It's unbelievable how long some people hold out, though. I reckon it's a kind of bloody-mindedness. But then Einar's family had a reputation for being stubborn. Determined not to give in but to go on battling the elements until the day they die.' After a brief pause, he added: 'Sorry, I didn't mean literally.'

Hulda decided not to encourage him by responding to this.

'I sometimes wondered if it was to do with money, you know? Maybe they just couldn't afford to move. I doubt the property would fetch much if it was sold, it's such poor grazing land. It wouldn't occur to anyone to start a farm there now. They would have to be crazy even to consider it. And the house is in a pretty dilapidated state, to be honest.'

'We'll soon see for ourselves,' Hulda said, a little sharply.

'Of course, it's been nothing but tragedy with that family –'

Hulda's patience was running out. She wanted to form an opinion of the case herself without having to listen to the inspector's theories. 'Are we nearly there?' she interrupted him.

'Nearly, not far now,' he answered in a rather subdued tone, having finally grasped that silence might be what Hulda was after.

*

In the event, though, the silence Hulda had been longing for brought no relief. Instead of providing her with the peace and quiet to clear her head in preparation for the investigation, it merely gave her more time to brood on thoughts of Dimma and her suicide, the gut-wrenching discovery of her body, the hazy ensuing hours and days, and the corrosive feeling of hatred for Jón, although she hadn't accused him of anything and he hadn't confessed.

That, and the questions that plagued her mercilessly: *Why didn't I do anything? Why didn't I see what was coming? Why didn't I stop him?*

Anyone would have thought Hulda the policewoman was a completely different person from Hulda the wife and mother: the former a tough nut who fought her corner; the latter a soft touch, gullible, passive. It was her cowardice, her sheer bloody cowardice, that had cost her so dear. She had never had the courage to tackle the situation head on. If she had done so, she might have realized what was going on behind closed doors.

'So, here we are,' the inspector said, trying to sound upbeat. Ahead of them, a house took shape through the falling snow. It was a traditional whitewashed Icelandic farmhouse, sitting huddled on its mound, the oldest part a low-rise wooden building clad in corrugated iron; the newer annex built of concrete, with dormer windows indicating an attic. The roof, swept bare of snow by the wind, was red and could have done with a fresh coat of paint. It was an exceptionally lonely-looking house. Even the farm buildings were tucked out of sight in a fold of the land. As they drove up the track they passed a rusty green jeep, parked some way below the house, which the inspector explained had belonged to the couple. Nature-lover though she was, Hulda would never have dreamt of living in such a bleak, isolated spot, especially not in the depths of winter. The solitude was almost palpable. The only other house she had seen on the way there had been a newer, slightly more hospitable-looking place, with blue walls and roof, a couple of kilometres back down the road.

There was a police car parked in the yard and, as the inspector drew up beside it, a young uniformed officer appeared on the doorstep of the farmhouse and gave them a friendly wave.

Hulda was the first out of the car, obeying an urgent need to get out into the fresh air, in spite of the snow. The car journey had left her feeling queasy and depressed.

Inspector Jens followed her up to the house, obviously keen not to miss anything.

'I'll come in with you,' he said, pushing past his subordinate to show Hulda inside. The air indoors was unpleasantly heavy, with that familiar, cloying odour that told Hulda a body had been lying there for some time. 'He's upstairs,' Jens said. They entered a plain, strikingly clean and tidy hall, which led into a sitting room. Here Hulda paused a moment. A desiccated Christmas tree drooped in one corner, its needles scattered over the floor and the small collection of parcels arranged underneath it. Clearly, the terrible events must have happened in the run-up to Christmas.

There was a pile of books on a little side table, revealed

by the labels on their spines to be library books. Beside them was a cup still half full of dark liquid and, on the larger table, there were two other cups, both empty. Hulda took a quick glance into the small kitchen that adjoined the sitting room. There were saucepans on the cooker but, apart from that, there was no obvious mess. Perhaps someone had tidied up for Christmas.

She went back into the sitting room and from there into a passage lined with four doors and a staircase to the attic. 'Up here,' the inspector informed Hulda solemnly, although he had already told her the body was upstairs. But, of course, she reminded herself, there was more than one body.

She accompanied the inspector up the stairs, doing her best to ignore the smell, refusing to let herself dwell on the fact that, only two months after finding the body of her daughter, she was about to be confronted by another corpse. She had never been hampered in her job by any squeamishness. But now she had an odd, vertiginous sensation, as if she were standing in the middle of a glacier, almost blinded by the glare of sunlit snow whichever way she looked, while ahead a crack had formed in the ice-sheet, a deep crevasse that was drawing ever closer. And she was falling . . .

At the top there was a narrow landing with three doors. One stood open and the inspector ushered Hulda towards it. Inside, the source of the throat-catching stench was revealed: the body of a middle-aged man lay on its back on the floor, a large patch of dried blood beside it. There was no sign of a weapon.

'That's Einar,' Jens said redundantly, after a respectful moment of silence. 'Sorry, it *was* Einar. The farmer.'

'Right. It doesn't look good, to be honest,' Hulda said. 'Though of course my colleagues will do a more thorough examination.'

'Yes, but you do agree it looks like murder, don't you?'

Hulda was struck by a suspicion that the inspector wanted it to be murder, that he was eager for the chance to work on a major crime. But maybe she was doing him an injustice. Was it age that had made her so cynical? Or was it what had happened at Christmas?

'Well, it doesn't appear to have been an accident, at any rate,' she said quietly. Something terrible had happened there, that much was plain.

'Shall we go back downstairs?'

Hulda lingered a moment, surveying the room. It was reasonably spacious, despite the low ceiling. In the corner under the dormer window was an old divan bed with a small table and lamp next to it, and a little bookcase under the sloping roof. Apart from the shocking aberration of the body lying in the middle of the floor, it seemed to have been quite a pleasant room, typical guest accommodation, neutral but homely.

What had the farmer been doing up here?

'OK, let's go downstairs,' she said. 'I've seen all I need to for the moment. By the way, what about these other rooms? Do you know what's in them?' She preferred not to check for herself as she didn't want to risk destroying any evidence before her colleagues had had a chance to carry out their examination.

'Yes, I had a look inside when we arrived, but they're just storerooms, so I closed the doors again. Downstairs there are three bedrooms and a bathroom. I took a quick peek in all of them, just to make sure there was no one else in the house. And there wasn't.'

'Thanks, my colleagues will conduct a more thorough investigation.'

She followed him down the narrow stairs.

'Now we have to go out in the cold, I'm afraid.'

Hulda still had her thick down jacket and gloves on. As they emerged on to the steps, she pulled a woolly hat from her pocket.

'It's not very far,' the inspector said. 'Just round that corner and down to the cellar.'

'Oh?' Hulda paused.

'Sorry, the original report we sent to Reykjavík may have been a bit garbled, but the second body is in the cellar.'

Hulda followed him down a set of steep steps that had been turned into a treacherously slippery slope by impacted ice and snow. The windowless cellar was illuminated by a single, low-watt light bulb, but the dim illumination was enough to reveal the body of a middle-aged woman lying against one wall.

'Erla, Einar's wife.'

This time there was no blood, but the scene was somehow even more gruesome than the first. The cold, drab, enclosed space gave Hulda a creeping sense of claustrophobia. She halted just inside the door, unable to make herself go any further.

'Of course, we don't know what happened here,' the inspector said, 'but there are various clues to suggest a violent death. A blow to the head, or strangulation, maybe. We'll soon find out.'

'Was it just the two of them here, as far as you know?' Hulda asked, cutting across his speculation.

'Yes, just them.'

'OK, let's go back outside.' Hulda was holding her breath. 'Get some air.'

'The smell, yes,' said the inspector, putting a hand to his nose.

'You get used to it,' Hulda said, once they were out in the open. Don't think about Dimma, she told herself. She tried to imagine that Hulda the detective was not the same woman as the one who had found her daughter dead on Christmas Day. She had to separate out these two sides of her life if she were to maintain her detachment. It was the only way she could carry on working, or indeed carry on at all.

In an effort to distract herself, she turned her attention to the surrounding countryside. The snow had stopped and the setting, now that she could see it, had a desolate sort of beauty under its light covering of white. The contrast between this pure, untouched landscape and the sordid scenes inside couldn't have been greater. The inspector had told her that the sheep had starved to death in the barn and that the scene that met the police there had been no less harrowing than the ones inside the house.

'Weren't there three of them?' Hulda asked.

'Three? The couple lived alone.'

'I mean, didn't they have a visitor?'

'Not at this time of year. That's completely out of the question. Nobody would come up here. Not –'

'Not even a guest for Christmas?'

'I very much doubt it. The road's usually blocked in December and the snow ploughs don't come this far up the valley, so it would mean covering a fair distance on foot.'

'So not completely out of the question, then?' Hulda asked carefully.

'No, of course not completely – it's just a manner of speaking – but I could swear they were alone here. They sometimes had visitors in the summer, and maybe in the spring and autumn too – they ran a sort of farm stay, or maybe that's not quite the right word . . .'

'How do you mean?'

'They invited young people to stay here in return for working on the farm – as cheap labour, you know. That's no way to run things, in my opinion, but then I'm old-fashioned.'

'It sounds like a perfectly sensible idea to me,' Hulda said, not hesitating to contradict the inspector, who was increasingly getting on her nerves. But maybe that was because she was letting everything get to her at the moment; her concentration was shot and her mind refused to stay on the job.

'Anyway, what made you wonder if there were three of them?' Jens asked.

'The three coffee cups in the sitting room.'

'Maybe they didn't bother to clear up every time they used a cup.'

'Well, we'll find out once we've lifted fingerprints from them. But, apart from that, the kitchen was very tidy, as if they were the types who put things away,' she replied dismissively. 'Besides, it doesn't work, does it? I mean, who killed who?'

'What? Oh, no, right, I see what you're getting at, of course,' Jens said, though Hulda suspected he had only just cottoned on. He frowned, then added: 'It's a hell of a situation – a hell of a situation.'

'If Einar attacked his wife, who murdered him?' Hulda asked rhetorically.

'Quite.'

'And if Erla attacked Einar, who killed her?'

'Quite,' Jens repeated, and stood there, brow furrowed. 'Unless one of them committed suicide?'

'Shall we take another look inside?' Hulda suggested, and started back without waiting for an answer.

The inspector followed a little way behind. Eventually he asked: 'Where is he, then?'

She paused and looked round enquiringly.

'Where is he, then – the other man, the third person?'

'We'll find out, don't you worry,' she said, the air of quiet authority in her voice disguising the fact that she wasn't at all sure her theory was correct or that she would ever identify the mysterious visitor. She mustn't lose faith in herself, though. She had to keep believing, as she tried to every day at work, that she was better than her male colleagues and that there was nothing she couldn't achieve.

It felt eerie going back into the house, where a quite literally deathly silence hung in the air and even the most ordinary, everyday objects took on a sinister appearance in light of what had happened. There were the three coffee cups, which her colleagues would take away for further analysis. And the stairs to the attic – Hulda had no intention of going back up there. She told herself it was because she wanted to let the experts do their job, but, if she were honest, it was because she would resort to any excuse to avoid seeing that grisly scene again, with its echoes of that other, more personal tragedy.

There were four rooms opening off the passage downstairs. The bathroom was stuck in a seventies time-warp with its yellow suite, green and yellow tiles, slightly damp-smelling carpet and the single bottle of Old Spice on one shelf. There were no signs of a struggle, no blood smears on the taps or sink, or anything else untoward. Then there was the master bedroom. At least, Hulda assumed this had been the couple's room. The double bed was large and hadn't been made, and two people usually slept there, as was apparent from the wrinkled sheets and the twin bedside tables, a pair of reading glasses on each.

The third room appeared to be a spare room, containing a single bed and a wardrobe, but there was no sign that anyone had been in there, and the air that met Hulda when she opened the door was stale and dry, as if no one had used it in a very long time.

The last room. Another spare room, she guessed, but something felt different about this one; she immediately sensed that someone had been there. There was a dressing table and a chest of drawers with a crowd of photographs on top, but Hulda didn't have time to pay any attention to these because her gaze was fixed on the bed. Somebody had slept in it: the pillow was dented and the bed hadn't been properly made.

Hulda turned round. The inspector was hovering in the passage, trying not to disturb her concentration. 'This is where their visitor slept,' she told him, feeling compelled to share the information as evidence of her theory. 'Someone's used the bed, see? There was a third person here over Christmas. Otherwise, I can't believe the bed wouldn't have been made. It seems out of character when the rest of the place is so tidy.'

He nodded, then a thought struck him. 'Unless the couple slept in separate beds . . . But, assuming you're right, where is he?'

'That's the question.'

Hulda went back outside, the inspector close on her heels. She needed to fill her lungs with cold, clean air to get rid of the sickening odour of decomposing flesh and clear her mind of the images of the dead: the farmer, his wife . . . and Dimma . . .

II

Erla got the shock of her life when she saw who it was.

It felt as if her heart had stopped beating, as if she were already dead. Then she came to her senses and felt genuinely afraid that this was the end. There was an unhinged look in his eyes; the mask had fallen.

It wasn't Einar.

It was the intruder, Leó.

Einar? Oh God, where was he?

Leó grabbed her roughly, without a word, a violent hatred in his eyes, and, strangely, despair.

Then it came back to her. She remembered where Einar was — lying in a dark pool of blood in the attic; dead, gone. She had been so sure she'd been hallucinating and that he was still alive; that it was just the two of them here. But now, horrifyingly, she knew she had been wrong.

Leó had her arm in an agonizing grip. He took a few steps into the darkness, dragging her with him. It came back to her with a sudden clarity that she had fled down to the cellar to hide from him.

She'd had some mad idea of using the spades or other tools for self-defence.

But now she was utterly powerless, unable to move, unable to do anything to prevent what was about to happen.

III

Hulda was sitting in the big police vehicle with the inspector, who had turned on the engine to get the heater going full blast. Her colleagues from Forensics were inside the house, conducting their painstaking investigation.

'We have to work on the basis that someone else was there with them,' Hulda said in a level voice, making an effort to be polite. She needed to cooperate with this man if she were to benefit from his local knowledge.

'Mm, yes, right,' he said warily.

'How far is it to the nearest neighbours? Is it possible that one of them could have come round for a visit . . . and that it ended badly?'

'Neighbours?' The inspector smiled. 'They didn't have any neighbours.'

'What do you mean?'

'The couple's nearest neighbours were the villagers, including me. All the other farms in this valley have been abandoned.'

'Well, supposing someone had come up from the village?'

'Like I said, no one came out here in winter, not a soul. No one had any business here and the couple didn't mix much with the villagers. They were well suited, Einar and Erla. They looked out for each other, if you know what I mean?'

Hulda was irritated by his presumptions. 'We can't rule anything out,' she said sharply. 'There are always exceptions.'

'Yes, of course, of course . . .'

'And the person in question could have driven – what – at least halfway here, from what you said earlier?'

'Yes, or maybe more, but they'd have had to walk the rest of the way. And the weather's unpredictable in these parts.'

Hulda thought about the parcels, the tree . . . The tragic events must have happened shortly before, or even during, the festivities. 'What was the weather like at Christmas?'

The inspector didn't even need to think. 'We had a violent storm right through the holiday, a complete white-out. The power went in the village, which means it must have gone up here too. It wasn't fixed until 26 December.' He sighed.

'A power cut, you say? Do you remember exactly when it happened?' Hulda pictured the darkness, wondering if it had fallen after the events, or whether it could have played a part in what had happened here. It was a chilling thought.

'Yes, I certainly do. It was on the twenty-third. The worst possible timing. We had a bloody nightmare trying to cook Christmas dinner the next day and missed the radio greetings, the carol service and everything. Old Ásgrímur at the Co-op had to open up on the evening of the twenty-third so people could buy batteries, candles and matches, and so on. I believe he completely ran out of batteries.'

'And the storm? When did that hit?'

'The weather was pretty bad during Advent – with a heavy snowfall but no actual blizzard. It was manageable, you know. Then a severe storm blew up at around the same time as the electricity went.'

'Could anyone have reached this place on foot in those conditions?'

'No, I'm absolutely sure they couldn't,' he said with conviction. 'It would have been impossible. There was an emergency storm warning. The wind was so strong you could barely stand up outside and there was a total white-out – zero visibility.'

'And it lasted until the twenty-sixth, you say? That's when the power came back on?'

'Thereabouts, yes.'

'So their visitor must have arrived by the twenty-third at the latest.'

'Yes, either then or after Christmas.'

'Hardly, since they were already dead by then. Their Christmas presents hadn't been opened.'

'Oh, yes, right. Now you mention it,' he said, wrongfooted.

'Could we drive back now?' she asked.

'Back? But your colleagues haven't finished.'

'They'll be fine. We'll pick them up later.'

'Where do you want to go?' he asked.

'Just to the point our mysterious visitor could have reached in the days before Christmas. To where he'd have been forced to leave his car.'

'OK, yes, sure, we can drive there. Though I didn't notice any car by the road.'

'We weren't specifically looking, though.'

'But surely it wouldn't still be there? He'd have made his getaway.'

'Maybe. But, who knows, there might be signs that a vehicle was parked there. Frozen ruts under the snow, for example.'

'True,' he said. 'OK. I'll just go and tell the boys where we're going.'

They drove for a while without speaking. Jens had obviously learned his lesson and Hulda had nothing to say to him. Nevertheless, after a few minutes she began to find the silence burdensome. The moment her attention wandered, Dimma would be there, waiting. Hulda had failed her. She had realized too late. The knowledge was searing, agonizing. She could feel herself developing a splitting headache as her daughter's name echoed louder and louder in her mind, until, unable to bear it any longer, she had to say something.

'Have . . . have you lived here long?'

'What, me? Never lived anywhere else. You get the

hang of village life; it's addictive, really. There's always something to keep you occupied, you know – hobbies, and so on . . .'

From his tone, Hulda gathered that he was waiting for her to ask him more about his hobbies. She supposed it could do no harm to oblige him.

'Oh, I see, like what, exactly?'

'Well, music, obviously.'

'Er, obviously?'

'Yes, you know, my song.'

She hadn't a clue what he was talking about but didn't like to ask.

Seeing her puzzlement, he looked embarrassed. 'Oh, sorry, I thought maybe you'd know it. Most people do, though I say so myself.' He mentioned a popular hit from the early seventies, a song Hulda was certainly familiar with.

'Was that you?'

'Indeed it was – the sins of my youth, and all that. I was the original one-hit wonder. But people are still always asking me to sing it.' He laughed. 'On the unlikeliest occasions. And at most get-togethers, you know. I usually give in – belt it out and strum along on the guitar.'

Looking at the stout, middle-aged man beside her, Hulda had trouble picturing him as a pop star. To her extreme annoyance, the chorus was now stuck in her head.

'I've got a sort of deal going with the restaurant in the village too. Well, restaurant's putting it a bit strong, it's more of a glorified petrol-station café really, where people go if they want a burger and chips, that sort of thing.

If there's a good crowd in, I sometimes sing for the diners and, in return, I get a free meal – singing for my supper, you know!' He chuckled. 'No doubt you'll pop in there yourself when you get a moment.'

Silence descended again after the confessions of the one-time pop star. Hulda contemplated the inhospitable landscape. The sky was threatening more snow. However picturesque the mountains and valley looked in their winter costume, she would never have dreamt of living out here. It might be a good area for hiking in summer, though.

It occurred to her that she hadn't been hiking in a long time. Perhaps that's what she needed: to head into the mountains and heal her wounded spirits in the great outdoors instead of being cooped up at home or working herself into the ground. There was no chance of that now, though. She needed to solve this case first, preferably with distinction.

Recalling a remark the inspector had made earlier, Hulda said: 'You mentioned that no one had been able to get hold of them on the phone, which was why you decided to come up here yourself to check on them. Was their phone working, did you happen to notice?'

'No, it was dead when I tried to ring them, as if there was something wrong with the phone or the line. But I forgot to check if there was a dialling tone while I was at the house.'

'Could you look into it later?'

'Of course, will do.'

*

'This is where the road usually gets blocked.' The inspector pulled up and they both got out of the car.

Hulda turned in a slow circle, taking in their surroundings.

'There, look,' she said after a moment, pointing off to one side. 'There's a vehicle of some kind. Looks like a big four-wheel drive.' The car was parked some way from the road.

'Yes, damn it, you're right. I didn't notice it before. The driver's taken a strange route, but . . . well, now you mention it . . . maybe . . .'

'Maybe what?' Hulda asked impatiently.

'Maybe it's understandable. I've often driven this way in winter. The road usually gets closed by heavy drifting at this point and they don't bother to plough any further. But a stranger to the area might make the mistake of thinking they could get round the blockage if they took a detour to the left. You can drive off the road here, if you've got the right sort of vehicle, because the ground is usually swept fairly bare by the wind. But it's deceptive. Our man would soon have got into trouble, I can swear to that. He'd have been stuck fast before he knew it.'

They both set off at a smart pace over the firm snow-crust towards the car. It was white, which had made it all the harder to see against the snowy backdrop, and Hulda couldn't immediately recognize the make, not from a distance. The inspector was quicker.

'Looks like a Mitsubishi. I've always wanted one of those myself.'

Hulda was just reflecting that she was quite happy with

her Skoda when she did a double-take and, glancing at the inspector, saw that he had been struck by the same thought, almost in the same instant.

'What the hell!' he said. 'It can't be . . .'

'A white Mitsubishi off-roader. My God!' Of course, they would have to confirm that it was the right licence number, but it couldn't be a coincidence.

'My God!' Hulda repeated. 'That's the very last thing I was expecting.'

IV

For obvious reasons, Hulda had never got round to returning the phone message from the parents of the missing girl on Christmas Day. She hadn't liked to disturb them that morning and at midday she had gone home, to be confronted by a scene of such unspeakable horror that her world had been turned upside down and she felt as if her life had effectively ended.

After the tragedy, it had naturally fallen to someone else to ring Unnur's parents back, if anyone had ever actually bothered. Later, though, when she started paying attention to the news again, Hulda guessed what the phone call had been about. It had transpired that Unnur's father had gone missing just before Christmas, without a word to his wife. His car had gone too. Hulda had been listening to the news in the distracted way she did everything these days, but this had caught her attention, since it had been her case. The father's disappearance, following that of his daughter, had caused quite a stir. All the evidence suggested that he had deliberately walked out. There was no reason to suspect foul play and no other obvious explanation. Hulda had drawn her own conclusions and assumed that her colleagues had done the same: the only logical explanation was that the father had been responsible for his daughter's death and that, unable to live with what he had done, he had taken his own life. The press hadn't said this in as many words but speculation about the case had been quietly allowed to die down, as if by consensus that this was a family tragedy and it would be inappropriate to delve too deeply.

The police investigation had drawn a complete blank, as if the man had vanished off the face of the earth. Hulda had guessed he'd probably driven his car off a cliff, but, as she'd been on compassionate leave at the time, she hadn't been party to the details of the case. At any rate, nothing had been seen or heard of him since.

Until now.

The father had driven off in a white Mitsubishi.

And now here they were, in the middle of nowhere, confronted with a car of that description.

'It has to be the right vehicle, doesn't it?' Hulda asked aloud, though she already knew the answer.

'Yes, it has to be. I got orders just after Christmas to keep an eye out for a white Mitsubishi – like all the other police stations in the country. I remember doing a circuit of the village, just in case, but I didn't spot anything and nothing I'd heard led me to expect the man to turn up on my patch. I've had no reason to come out this way until now . . . What on earth could he have been doing out here?'

'Well, that's far from clear, but I suppose it could –'

The inspector broke in: 'It has to be connected to his daughter, doesn't it?'

Hulda stood still, staring at the car.

What in God's name had Unnur's father been doing here?

'Yes, I think it must be,' she said at last.

'But she went missing on the other side of the country . . .'

'Yes, she was last heard of just outside Selfoss, which is certainly a long way from here . . . I really don't understand this.'

'Me neither . . . And now I'm bound to get a rap over the knuckles for not having combed the area better at the time,' said Jens gloomily, more to himself than to Hulda.

She didn't have the patience to reassure him. Her mind was entirely focused on the case at hand. Or cases, perhaps? Because surely this must constitute a proper lead at last in relation to Unnur's disappearance?

She scraped the snow off the windows and peered into the car, careful not to touch anything. Others would need to carry out a proper examination. But she was at least able to satisfy herself that there was no one inside. And there was nothing immediately obvious that could shed light on what had happened.

'Do you think he could have been with the couple over Christmas?' the inspector asked eventually.

Hulda thought about it. 'It has to be a possibility, though I can't begin to imagine why. But no one would have had any reason to come out this way, would they, except to visit them?'

'No, absolutely none. That would suggest that he walked from here to the farm. It's quite a hike, but not too difficult, as long as the visibility's OK.'

'Even if you don't know the area?'

'Yes, I'd say so. The road goes straight up to the head of the valley from here.'

'But it would be easy to go astray if there was a blizzard, wouldn't it?'

'I should think so. There aren't many landmarks to help you if you wander off the road, and there are plenty of old stories about travellers dying of exposure in these parts. Ghost stories, and so on. I wouldn't want to be caught here on foot myself if a storm blew up, I can tell you.'

Hulda started walking back towards the police car, deep in thought, and the inspector followed.

She hauled herself up into the passenger seat and, once the inspector was behind the wheel, she said: 'The man has to be around here somewhere . . . assuming this is his car. And I think we've pretty much established that he's not at the farm, don't you agree?'

'He can't possibly be there,' Jens confirmed, then added: 'Do you think he murdered the couple?'

Hulda didn't say anything for a moment. It was the only logical conclusion and yet she couldn't bring herself to say it aloud. She'd met the man several times in connection with Unnur's disappearance and had liked him. He'd come across as a polite, personable lawyer, a concerned father. And yet . . . there had been something in his manner that had made Hulda uneasy; she had sensed that in certain circumstances he might be capable of anything, that he was unpredictable. Could he in fact have murdered his daughter and then the couple on the farm? But why? It didn't make sense, didn't make sense at all . . .

'I don't think we can rule it out,' she said at last. 'That he's responsible for what happened here at Christmas, I mean.'

'Of course, there's always a chance . . .' Jens said slowly, pondering. Hulda waited impatiently for him to finish the sentence: '. . . a chance he's at the other house.'

'The one we drove past earlier?'

'Yes, no one lives there.'

'And what . . . just left his car sitting here all this time?'

'No, well, I don't know.'

Although Hulda wasn't convinced, it would be worth making absolutely sure.

'Shall we drive over and check it out?' the inspector asked hesitantly. Hulda was pleased to find him submitting so completely to her authority.

'Yes, let's do that,' she said firmly.

V

The blue paint was weathered on the walls and roof, and even under the quilt of snow it was apparent that the garden around the house had been left to run wild. When Hulda and the inspector tried the front door they found it unlocked, so there was nothing to stop them pushing it open and stepping inside.

There was no sign that anyone had been there recently, though the house was still fully furnished, with a sofa and armchairs in the sitting room, and a table and crockery in the kitchen, as if the last occupant had been intending to come back.

'There's only a single storey, but I think there's a cellar as well,' said Jens. 'I'll take a quick look down there, but it seems pretty clear to me that he can't have been here.'

Hulda nodded without speaking, and Jens vanished from view.

There was an odd atmosphere in this house, with its mute witnesses to the past, to a life someone had lived there not that long ago, yet not that recently either. A thick layer of dust coated all the surfaces. Hulda wandered from room to room and found that they all told the same story. There was a single bed in the bedroom, but no personal items. It could have been a guesthouse, waiting for visitors. She went back into the kitchen and opened the fridge, but it was empty and unplugged. When she pressed the light switch by the kitchen door, to her surprise, the bulb came on. The radiators turned out to be lukewarm as well, not enough to heat the house so you would notice but enough presumably to stop the pipes from freezing while the place was unoccupied. Clearly, this was a house with a history, perhaps an interesting one, but any curiosity she felt about that would have to wait. For the moment, the priority was to find out what had happened to the couple on the neighbouring farm and, no less important, what had become of Unnur's father, the lawyer Haukur Leó, known to his friends and family as Leó.

After they had found the abandoned Mitsubishi, Jens had radioed from the police car to get confirmation that it was indeed the vehicle the police had been searching for. The discovery had turned the whole case upside down – both cases, in fact: the tragic events at the farm, on the one hand, and the disappearance of Unnur and her father on the other. It stood to reason that there had to be a link, if only Hulda could work it out.

'The cellar was locked, but I took the liberty of forcing the door,' Jens told her. 'It wasn't very difficult. I'll see that it's repaired later.'

'Did you find anything?'

The inspector shook his head. 'Not a thing. Where the hell is this guy?'

'We'll have to organize a search,' Hulda said, aware that time was working against them. The trail had long gone cold and she would have to do everything in her power to blow life back into any faint embers that could possibly light her way. Her primary concern, though, was to find Unnur, the girl she'd been searching for since the autumn. If there was any hope, however faint, that she could still be alive, Hulda *had* to save her.

Or at least do her level best.

VI

Unnur didn't make it any further than Kirkjubæjarklaustur that first day.

This was exactly how her journey was meant to be, a mixture of uncertainty and adventure. But she had no particular desire to get stuck in this quiet little south Iceland town, located in the green oasis between the two great icecaps of Mýrdalsjökull and Vatnajökull. She was after a different kind of experience, one which involved seeking out remote places and dramatic scenery, not holing up in a town or village. At present she was sitting in a small café attached to a petrol station.

The driver of the BMW who had picked her up hadn't been going any further for the moment. He had turned out to be a foreigner, a friendly, middle-aged German office worker who had long dreamt of visiting Iceland. They had chatted all the way. Since she loved meeting new people and gaining an insight into their lives, she was very satisfied with her journey so far.

The question was, where next?

She thought she'd take the bus but didn't know where to yet, except that it would have to be east. She didn't want to retrace her route west towards Selfoss and Reykjavík as it would feel too much like a backward step, like throwing in the towel. Instead, she felt compelled to go on, into the unknown.

It was quiet in the café. Unnur had treated herself to a coffee and a cold sandwich, both of which were pretty uninspiring. The coffee was at least hot, though, and the sandwich was edible, so it would have to do.

On the table next to her was a pile of advertising leaflets and a day-old newspaper. She began by leafing through the paper but soon gave up as there was something rather depressing about getting dragged back into the same old political bickering. She had deliberately avoided the news recently, paying no particular attention to what was going on in the world.

Laying aside the paper, she glanced absent-mindedly at the advertising brochures, some in colour, others in black and white, which were mostly aimed at Icelandic tourists exploring their own country. At the bottom of the pile was a photocopied sheet that Unnur paused to read, perhaps because it was so appealingly old-fashioned and amateurish. It turned out to be an advertisement for volunteers to work on a farm in return for board and lodging.

Like many Icelanders, she had spent a couple of summers on a farm as a little girl, helping out with the chores and experiencing traditional life in the countryside, but it had never occurred to her to do it again once she had grown up. Still, this was too exciting an opportunity to pass up; it was exactly the sort of experience she pictured as being both interesting and different – a glimpse into a vanishing way of life. And the free board and lodging would help to eke out her savings.

The photocopied sheet provided the basic facts, including directions for how to find the place, which involved taking a bus to a village in the east. The farm itself was quite a distance beyond the village; a bit of a trek on foot, it said, but a lift could be arranged. She immediately made up her mind to walk; what a dream that would be.

There was a phone number at the bottom of the sheet. It would be silly to travel all the way out east without ringing ahead, only to discover that the place was no longer available. Grabbing the advertisement, she went over to the counter, leaving her coffee and sandwich behind on the table, confident that no one would bother to steal them.

'Excuse me,' she said to the teenage boy who was on duty that evening on the till.

'Mm?'

'Excuse me, could I use your phone?'

The boy rolled his eyes. 'There's a payphone round the back — there, look . . .' He pointed to the left. 'Behind that wall.'

Unnur pulled out a hundred-krónur note. 'Could you change this for me?'

The boy hesitated, as if thinking of refusing, then took the note with a long-suffering air, opened the till and gave her a shower of ten-krónur pieces.

Unnur quickly found the phone and dialled the number.

VII

They were sitting in the inspector's office at the village police station.

The office was on the small side, like the station itself, but Jens had made it homely. There were family photos on a shelf and the room was notably tidy; the desk wasn't buried in an avalanche of papers like Hulda's. Perhaps this was the result of less pressure and fewer cases, or perhaps Jens was just naturally more organized.

Now that he was on home ground, comfortably enthroned behind his desk, while Hulda perched on the hard visitor's chair, it seemed their roles had been reversed.

The media had got wind of the deaths, upping the pressure a little. A reporter from the State Broadcaster had rung the police station and Jens had chosen to field the call himself rather than passing it on to Hulda. She'd caught snippets of what the caller was saying but had been too slow to intervene. Her immediate reaction would have been to say 'No comment', but Jens was clearly enjoying the limelight. In fact, he was so busy basking in his five minutes of fame that he blurted out far too much information. Mercifully, it was too late to make the main evening news on TV, but the report would doubtless make it on to the ten o'clock radio bulletin. Hulda could only hope the papers wouldn't get hold of it in time to make a splash tomorrow morning. She could do with a little more breathing space. To be fair to Jens, though, he hadn't given away the fact that the police suspected murder, merely confirmed the discovery of two bodies. That alone was enough to generate a huge amount of interest but, in Hulda's experience, when it came to cases like this, Icelandic journalists could usually be trusted to respect the interests of the investigation. Fortunately, Jens hadn't revealed the possible link between the current incident and the mysterious disappearances of Haukur Leó and his daughter, Unnur, either.

They were waiting in his office for the head of the local search-and-rescue team, who was on his way to meet them.

Hulda heard a noise outside in the corridor and, glancing round, saw a lean, bespectacled figure appear in the doorway. 'Hello there.' She judged him to be around thirty, ten years younger than her. He entered the room briskly, held out his hand and introduced himself: 'I'm Hjörleifur. I take care of search-and-rescue operations in the area.'

'Hello. I'm Hulda, from Reykjavík CID,' she said. 'Thanks for coming. We need to organize a search for a man.'

'Yes, so I gathered.' Hjörleifur remained standing, as there weren't any free chairs in the little office. 'Jens mentioned that when he rang me. We're talking about the man who went missing at Christmas, right?'

'That's right,' Jens said, with self-conscious solemnity.

'Sure, of course we can do it,' Hjörleifur replied.

He looked from Jens to Hulda.

'When can you start?' she asked. 'How long will it take to call out your members?'

'Call out our members? That won't take long, but it's coming down heavily out there now and it's dark too, so we won't be going anywhere in a hurry. If the man's out there, his body must have been lying there since Christmas, so surely a day or two more isn't going to make any difference?'

Hulda rose from her chair, fixing Hjörleifur with a stern gaze and saying emphatically: 'On the contrary, it's extremely urgent. We're looking for a girl who's been missing since last autumn. We don't know what happened to her, but we've finally picked up her trail. If there's the slightest chance she might still be alive . . .'

Hjörleifur was momentarily too disconcerted by her vehemence to answer. Then he nodded. 'OK, fine, I'll assemble the team. But I hope you're not expecting to find the man alive.'

'I'd be surprised,' Hulda said in a more composed voice, sitting down again. 'Can you start straight away?'

'Not in the dark, but as soon as it's light tomorrow,' Hjörleifur muttered, sounding rather sheepish now. 'But, just to be clear, if conditions get significantly worse, we'll have to abort the search. We're not taking any risks.'

'We understand that,' Jens said.

From his tone, Hulda wasn't sure if he was on her or Hjörleifur's side. Perhaps it was foolhardy to insist on sending out a search party to comb the countryside for a body in this weather, but the girl's disappearance had touched a nerve with her and she wanted to pull out all the stops to solve the case. Not that she was kidding herself that there would be any happy ending.

'Then I'd better get going, since there's obviously no time to lose,' Hjörleifur said, not even trying to disguise the sarcasm in his voice. He took his leave of them.

'Hadn't we better go back up to the farm?' Hulda asked, turning to Jens. She was feeling far too restless to wait around with nothing to do.

'Are you sure? It'll mean having to drive all the way out there and back again tonight. My lads could give your colleagues a lift once they've finished.' His lack of enthusiasm was obvious.

Hulda nodded. 'Quite sure. I'd like to be there personally to hear how they're getting on with the crime-scene investigation.'

This time the drive was more arduous, as snow had drifted over the road since that morning. Hulda spared a guilty thought for the rescue-team members who were going to have to scour the valley and moors in these conditions.

When they finally reached the farmhouse, Hulda's colleagues were just finishing up. They had taken samples and photographs and reckoned they had enough evidence to be going on with.

They had made one unexpected discovery: it was plain

that someone had deliberately sabotaged the telephone connection by pulling out some of the wires, then hiding the evidence. 'It wouldn't have required any expert knowledge and would probably only have taken a minute,' Hulda was told when she asked for details. In addition, a preliminary analysis of the fingerprints on the coffee cups had confirmed her theory that there had been three people in the house.

Both bodies had already been removed by ambulance and the rescue team weren't due to begin their search from the farm until the following morning. It was agreed, therefore, that the two police vehicles should travel back to the village in convoy, but there was something Hulda wanted to do first.

'Is it all right for me to go in now and take a closer look around?' she asked one of her colleagues from Forensics. He nodded.

She had a disorientating sensation of walking into a painting: a cosy sitting room in a house where no one lived any more, where the clock seemed to have stopped at Christmas, although it was now well into February. It was as if the house were caught in some strange limbo: there were signs of life everywhere you looked, yet the air was tainted by the smell of death, a reminder that the Grim Reaper had recently wielded his scythe there. She tried to visualize the scene. Had all three of them – the farming couple and Haukur Leó – sat here together in the days before Christmas? Had he been a complete stranger to them? If so, what was he doing here in the middle of winter? Or could the couple have been relatives?

It had occurred to Hulda while she was at the police station that she should seize the chance to ring his wife, Unnur's mother, and let her know that the Mitsubishi had been found. This would have given her an excuse to ask the woman about any possible link to the couple out east. Yet she had hesitated, preferring to wait until she had made a bit more progress with the investigation. Until she could put the poor woman out of her misery by telling her straight that her husband was dead – and perhaps give her news of her daughter at the same time.

That conversation would have to wait until tomorrow at the earliest, unless there were any unexpected developments tonight.

Hulda walked past the stairs to the attic since she simply didn't have the mental strength to go up there again just yet. Subconsciously, she knew that this was because, apart from the blood, the scene had been too grim a reminder of her own private trauma.

Instead, she revisited the couple's bedroom. Jens had suggested they might have slept in separate rooms as a possible explanation for the fact that both the double bed and the bed in the guestroom had been used. Now, though, there was compelling evidence that his theory was wrong: a third person had been there – Haukur Leó must have been staying with them. As further proof that the couple had slept together, there were, as Hulda had noticed earlier, two pairs of reading glasses. There was also a half-empty water glass on one bedside table, along with a novel, Halldór Laxness's *Salka Valka*, the bookmark revealing that the reader hadn't got very far with it.

Apart from that, it was rather a cheerless room, Hulda felt. Impersonal, somehow. She couldn't immediately work out what it was that gave that impression, then recalled the photographs on the chest of drawers in the spare room. That was it: there were no family pictures in here. Of course, that wasn't necessarily significant, but it seemed odd, all the same.

Hulda left the couple's room and went back into the spare room, where Haukur Leó had presumably slept. There were the family photos, all in one place. Hulda had given them a cursory glance when she examined the room the first time round but now she stopped to consider them more closely. Her attention was arrested by one particular snapshot in the middle. It showed the couple, Erla and Einar, probably in their thirties, looking young and care-free, and between them a pretty, red-haired girl in her teens . . . And . . . there was something about the girl that struck Hulda; yes, she reminded her a little of Unnur, the missing girl from Gardabær. Maybe it was just that Hulda was preoccupied by both cases, and yet there was a resemblance. They were both redheads, of course, but it was more than that; they were actually quite alike.

She wondered who the girl in the picture was and guessed she must be the couple's daughter; the atmosphere in the photo certainly gave that impression, since they both had their arms around her, and Hulda's immediate assumption had been that this was a family portrait.

But if so, where was the girl now?

And why had nobody mentioned her?

*

Inspector Jens was standing outside in the driving snow, buffeted by the wind, which seemed unrelenting in this exposed spot.

'Could I have a word?' Hulda asked, but he continued to stare into space. Walking over, she tapped him on the shoulder and he jumped.

'I wanted to ask you something.'

'Sorry, I didn't hear you. Should we go inside?'

She nodded and they returned to the welcome shelter of the hall.

'I was looking at the photographs – the family photos, you know – and there was one of the couple with a young girl. Did they have a daughter?'

'Yes,' the inspector answered promptly: 'Anna.' His expression grew sombre.

'Where is she?'

This time it took him longer to reply: 'She lived on the neighbouring farm, in the blue house we visited earlier.'

'She lived there? Then where is she now?' Hulda pictured the rooms in the empty house, the home that someone seemed to have left in a hurry, never to return.

'She's dead,' Jens said heavily.

'Dead? But . . . she must have died very young.' Hulda tried hard to focus, to keep her thoughts from straying to Dimma, but she could hear her voice breaking.

'Very. She was no more than twenty, if I remember right. She'd just moved home again after finishing sixth-form college. Well, not exactly home: she moved into the old tenant farm, as I said. It caused quite a stir in the village. Most people had taken it for granted she'd move south to Reykjavík and do something different with her life. But the countryside exerts a strong pull. It was in her blood. I remember bumping into her not long after she moved home, and she was radiant with happiness. She lived for this place.'

Hulda was feeling too choked up to continue with the conversation. All she could see was Dimma, and she knew that any minute now she would break down in tears. The only way she could hide them was outside in the falling snow. Yet, clearing her throat, she forced herself to ask, trying to keep the quiver out of her voice: 'What . . . what happened to Anna?' She had to know.

VIII

Unnur experienced an intoxicating feeling of pure, unadulterated freedom. She was as free as a bird, dependent on no one, all her belongings in her backpack – everything that mattered, at least; most importantly, her notebooks. Her writing was going well. And nobody knew where she was. She hadn't got round to telling her parents where she was heading next, as there was no urgency. She was taking a year's break from them as well. Of course, she loved them dearly, but this was her time and she was determined to manage on her own.

It had taken her a couple of days to get here. From Kirkjubæjarklaustur she had travelled by bus along the south coast to Höfn í Hornafirdi. It was one of the most spectacular roads in Iceland: to the south, there was nothing but the immense, flat ocean; on the landward side to the north, the vast Vatnajökull icecap with its jagged fringe of peaks and succession of glacial tongues, tumbling one after another down towards the plain. With the handful of other passengers – a few locals and a scattering of foreigners – she had got out to marvel at the intensely blue glacial lagoon at Jökulsárlón, with its jostling crowd of icebergs. Yet, stunning though the scenery was, the experience had made her feel like a tourist rather than an adventurer. She was impatient to get off the beaten track, leave behind the Ring Road with its famous sights and head up into the lonely valleys of the interior, where a few last farms were still clinging on.

After a night in the youth hostel at Höfn, Unnur had continued her journey by bus up the east coast, leaving the icecap behind and entering a new, green landscape of fjords and layer-cake mountains, finally arriving at the village the woman had mentioned on the phone. From there, she had kept to her plan of walking rather than trying to organize a lift. It was a fine day, with that extraordinary clarity that you only get in an Icelandic autumn, every ridge and gully standing out so clear in the pure air that it looked as if you could reach out and touch them. The hike took hours, but the exercise and the sensation of being completely alone, following a narrow ribbon of road up the uninhabited, treeless valley, left her feeling mentally and physically invigorated. She had brought along a packed lunch and perched on a rock beside the road to eat it. Close at hand, rugged fells rose above the green, U-shaped valley, and the only sounds to break the silence were the mournful calls of whimbrel and the gurgling of a stream.

Her backpack was beginning to weigh heavily on her shoulders by the time she finally spotted a house ahead. Her spirits lifted but were almost immediately dashed when she realized from the description she'd been given that it couldn't be the right place. So she kept going, further than she had thought possible, her pack heavier with each step, blisters forming on her feet, until the farmhouse appeared unexpectedly round a bend at the head of the valley. White with a red roof, as the woman had said, standing utterly alone on its mound, the only building to be seen in the wide, empty landscape. Unnur had the giddying sensation of having literally reached the edge of the inhabited world. This was exactly what she had been looking for.

Here, she would find the peace and quiet she craved. She could work during the day and write in the evenings, undisturbed by external distractions. She wondered if they even had TV reception out here, and hoped not. A quick scan of the roof established that there was no aerial.

Two or three weeks should be about right. That's what she'd agreed with the farmer's wife over the phone. Her name was Erla and, from her voice and manner, Unnur had got the impression she was a nice person.

Unnur trudged up to the front door, only to hesitate a moment before raising her fist to knock. This was her last chance to back out, she found herself thinking. But surely there was no reason to do that? She knocked and waited.

When the door opened she was greeted by a middle-aged woman who just stood there, studying her thoughtfully for a while, as if sizing her up. Eventually, she said: 'Hello. Welcome. I'm Erla. Do come in.'

Unnur followed Erla into the sitting room and noticed a cup of coffee on the table beside an open book.

'Your room's in the attic,' Erla said. 'The stairs are along here.' Then, after a pause, she added: 'But what am I thinking of? Can I offer you something to drink? Some coffee, perhaps? I didn't hear a car. Surely you haven't walked all the way?'

'Yes . . . yes, actually, I did walk,' Unnur said, a little shyly.

'Well I never. Then you'll definitely need some refreshment. You do drink coffee, don't you?' Erla asked, and Unnur got the impression that 'no' would not be an acceptable answer.

'Of course.'

'Have a seat, then. There's hot coffee in the pot.'

Unnur obeyed, gratefully taking off her backpack and sitting down on the sofa. She looked round the room, taking in the old, slightly shabby furniture, the grandfather clock that seemed to have stopped and the walls hung with amateurish landscape paintings and reproductions of well-known works. It was all a bit tired and worn, yet the overall effect was cosy.

Erla disappeared, then came straight back with the coffee.

'Here you are, dear. Strong, black and sugarless.' She paused, then added: 'Or do you take milk and sugar? I can fetch them.'

Unnur shook her head. 'This is fine, thanks.'

'You must be exhausted.'

'It was, er, quite good exercise,' Unnur said, taking a sip of the ferociously strong black brew.

'I'm alone here at the moment,' Erla told her. 'My husband's in Reykjavík. He often has to go at this time of year. So there's plenty to do. You won't have time to get bored.'

'Oh, right, that sounds good. Having enough to do, I mean.'

'You mentioned on the phone that you were writing a book,' Erla went on, staring at her with a peculiar intensity.

'Yes, or at least I'm trying to. In my free time.'

'Yes, well, there's plenty to do here, but plenty of free time too. Once the day's chores are over, our life here's pretty uneventful, unless you plan to walk into the village in the evenings.' She smiled. 'It's good to have something to occupy yourself with. I myself read, you know.'

Unnur nodded.

'Anyway, your room's upstairs. It's not very big but I hope it's all right. No one's complained so far.'

'Thanks, I'm sure it'll be great. I don't need many creature comforts.'

'That's just as well. I'm very pleased to have you here, by the way. It's a lonely spot, especially when Einar's away. I have a feeling we're going to get on well.'

Again, Unnur nodded.

'Our meals are pretty traditional – old-fashioned home cooking, you know the sort of thing. Country food, really.' Erla smiled again. 'It might be a bit different from what you're used to in . . .'

'Gardabær,' Unnur finished for her. 'I've never been a fussy eater, and, yes, I'm sure we'll get on well.'

IX

'It must have been about ten years ago,' Jens said, frowning. He and Hulda were still standing huddled in the hall, their hands buried in their pockets to keep warm. The inspector had pulled the door to but, even so, a cold draught was stealing in from outside. Hulda shivered involuntarily.

Jens thought for a moment, then went on: 'Yes, that's right, it would be about ten years since their daughter died.'

Hulda waited without speaking. She still didn't trust her voice.

'I only know the background from what I've heard from other people, but then, more or less everything gets around in the countryside. Anyway, as I said, their daughter moved home to the neighbouring farm after finishing college. Apparently, Erla was very upset.'

'Oh?'

'The gossip was that Erla had sent her daughter away to school as far from here as possible. It seems she was hoping Anna would settle in Reykjavík. Erla was from the city herself and was never happy here – I think most people would agree about that. She must have regretted leaving the capital and wanted to make sure her daughter would have the chances she herself had missed out on, if you know what I mean?'

'Yes.'

'But Anna knew her own mind. She wasn't going to let anyone tell her what to do. She loved the country life, like most of us who live here, so she moved back.'

Hulda nodded.

'Erla hated the isolation, the winters, the darkness – that was obvious when you met her. She always used to come into the library to stock up on books before winter really set in, and Gerdur, the librarian, remarked to me more than once that it felt like serving someone facing a prison sentence. You'd have thought she was on her way to do a stint in solitary confinement.' The inspector paused to reflect. 'I suppose Erla wanted to spare her daughter that kind of existence, but in reality she was trying to save her life, though neither she nor anyone else could have known that then, if you see what I mean?'

Again, Hulda nodded, though of course she didn't know what Jens was referring to.

'Was it Einar?' she blurted out, though she hadn't meant to say anything.

'What? Einar?'

'Was she trying to keep her daughter away from Einar?'

'You mean . . . ? Good grief, no! Einar wasn't like that. *Absolutely not.*'

Hulda lowered her eyes, her thoughts on Jón and

Dimma. Perhaps, deep down, she had been hoping that the story of Erla, Einar and Anna was somehow similar. That she wasn't the only one to have been in this situation.

'Well, then disaster struck,' Jens said, lowering his voice, as if reluctant to tell the story. 'It was winter, of course.' He sighed. 'The winters are very long out here, as you can imagine. Not only long, but we get a lot of snow. It happened in December, shortly before Christmas, as a matter of fact. The weather was about as bad as it can get. It had been snowing relentlessly.'

Hulda found it easy to picture the conditions. It would have been enough to take a quick peek outside the front door and imagine a bit more snow on the landscape.

'Anna was staying with her parents at the time. She'd come over to see them before the weather deteriorated and got stuck here. Anyway, she was going down to the cellar on some errand when she slipped on the ice, fell and hit her head on the edge of one of the concrete steps. Her parents didn't see the accident, but Erla found her, not long after she'd fallen, apparently. The girl was unconscious but still alive, though she'd lost a lot of blood. Of course, they immediately rang for an ambulance . . .'

He broke off and Hulda felt it best not to prompt him.

'I remember . . .' he said, his gaze unfocused, 'I remember so well how Erla described it. They didn't dare move her, so they crouched out there in the snow beside the girl and basically watched her die. It took a long time. They tried to stop the bleeding – they were given instructions over the phone – and managed to some extent, but it wasn't enough. Erla said she just sat there for ages, powerless to do anything. The thing was, you see, that –'

Hulda, guessing the rest, finished for him: 'The ambulance couldn't get through because the road was blocked.'

'Exactly. It did get here eventually, but it had to wait for the snow plough first. They even called out a helicopter, but the decision was taken too late. Anna was dead by the time the ambulance finally got here. The tragic part was that it would have been a simple matter to save her life if they could have got her to a doctor sooner.'

'So it was the isolation that killed her,' Hulda murmured.

'Yes. I'm told that's how Erla always saw it. Like I said, she'd become pretty disenchanted with life out here anyway, even before it happened, so you can just imagine how she felt about it after Anna's death. But instead of moving away, she stayed. She stuck by Einar. She changed, though, and became a bit peculiar.'

'In what way?'

'It was like she refused to accept what had happened. Of course, we don't know what she was like at home because Einar never spoke about it. He never was much of a talker, anyway. For him, actions spoke louder than words. And he'd never have gossiped about his wife. But she was a frequent visitor to the village and, more often than not, she'd talk about Anna as if she was still alive. I've heard stories from various people, in the library, the shop, and so on. Sometimes she'd even talk about how she was expecting Anna to come over later and was doing the shopping ready for her visit, that kind of thing. I don't suppose many people had the heart to correct her, so I get the impression she convinced herself Anna wasn't dead. She invented an alternative world in her head and lived in that, alongside the real one.' After a moment he added: 'And who can blame her?'

Hulda had tried to listen to the story with professional detachment but, every time he mentioned Anna, she found herself picturing Dimma. And now all she could think of was the frightening possibility that she, Hulda, might unravel in the same way as Erla; that she might retreat into some corner of her mind to escape – if only briefly – the unbearable pain that had been pursuing her like a shadow ever since that terrible moment on Christmas Day.

X

Her memories of Dimma's funeral were partly shrouded in fog, partly too starkly vivid, as if reflecting her simultaneous desire to remember and to forget. It was one of the hardest days of her life, and the weather, as if in sympathy, had been bitterly cold. There had been intermittent snow flurries and a fierce, blustery wind, as one might expect on the penultimate day of the year. Hulda had met the vicar two days earlier to go over the main points of her daughter's life with him but the meeting had ended prematurely when she'd broken down, too overcome with grief to continue. She hadn't met the vicar before. As the family weren't regular churchgoers, the task of conducting her daughter's funeral service had fallen to a stranger. Not that it had mattered. Nothing mattered any more.

The vicar had duly given the funeral address, but Hulda couldn't remember what he had said, since she hadn't taken anything in. Instead, she had found herself thinking about the address that would one day be given at her own funeral, whenever that might be.

Although she had sat in the pew beside Jón, there had been an invisible, impenetrable wall between them. They both knew that their daughter's death was entirely his fault. What he had done to her was so unforgiveable that it couldn't be put into words.

Sometimes Hulda found herself wishing that Dimma had left a suicide note, but at others she was extremely relieved that she hadn't. Such a letter would no doubt have been a severe indictment of both her parents; Jón for his crimes, Hulda for her complacency.

As the coffin was lowered into the ground on that bitterly cold day, Hulda's tears had melted the snow at her feet and the howling of the wind had echoed the scream inside her.

XI

It was nearly midnight. Hulda and Inspector Jens were once again on their way back to the village in the big police vehicle. Although the snow was still coming down, the flakes were wetter and no longer settling, which made the road easier to negotiate.

Hulda kept picturing the missing girl, Unnur, trying to persuade herself that she might still be alive, that it might still be possible to rescue her. She simply had to believe it.

She dreaded the night ahead. Nights were the most difficult time. Her sleep was fitful at best, disturbed by feverish dreams, but worst of all were the hours she lay awake, her head thrashing back and forth on the pillow, alone with her merciless thoughts. That was when she came closest to tipping over the edge.

And now the night was approaching with inexorable speed. Hulda would have preferred to remain at the scene and wait for news, passing the time by talking to Jens. She might even have been able to doze a bit and recharge her batteries that way.

'Are you building up a picture yet?' the inspector asked, his voice barely audible over the roar of the engine and the battering of the wind against the windows.

Hulda had to admit that much remained unclear. Judging by the evidence at the scene, they could be fairly certain that a third person had killed both husband and wife, for reasons that were obscure. They had also established that there had been another person with them in the house, and the odds were that this had been Haukur Leó. Otherwise, why on earth would his car have been abandoned there? The question was what had happened to him, and what possible reason could he have had for travelling right across the country to this remote spot just before Christmas?

Unnur.

There could be no other reason. He had to have been looking for his daughter.

But why here?

Did Unnur have some connection to the couple on the farm? None had emerged during the original inquiry following her disappearance, though the search had been very thorough and every possible clue had been followed up.

No, there wasn't any connection. Except the odd coincidence that the couple's daughter had borne a striking resemblance to Unnur. Was there any chance they had been related?

She would have to ring Unnur's mother when they got back to the village, however late the hour. The woman might be able to shed some light on what could have taken her husband to a remote farm in east Iceland, over 600 kilometres from home. And besides, she had every right to know that Haukur Leó's car had turned up.

Hulda sat on the bed in the little guesthouse where she had been provided with a room. It was clean but rather chilly, as if the owner were too mean to heat the rooms properly.

She had looked up Unnur's mother's number in the telephone directory. After sitting there for a while, mentally preparing herself, she went ahead and dialled it. The phone rang and rang before eventually the poor woman answered, her voice husky with sleep and anxiety.

'Hello, this is Hulda Hermannsdóttir, from CID,' she said formally, although there was no real need to give her full name since she had been a frequent visitor to the couple's home in the period following Unnur's disappearance.

'Hulda? Hello . . .'

Hulda heard the woman's sharp intake of breath as she realized what this could mean.

'I'm sorry to ring you so late. It's about your husband, Haukur Leó . . . We've found his car.'

'What, you've found it? But he . . . have you found him?'

'No, not yet. We're going to launch a search first thing in the morning.'

'Where . . . where was it?' the woman asked, her voice choked by tears.

'In the east,' Hulda told her, and proceeded to give a more detailed description of the location.

The woman's bewilderment was obvious. 'What . . .

why . . . what on earth was he doing there? I just don't understand.'

'Do either of you have any link to this area? The car was found near the farm of a couple called Einar and Erla. Are you familiar with those names?'

'We . . . we don't have any family out east. I've never . . . never heard of these people.'

'That's helpful to know. We're working round the clock to try and shed some light on the matter. It appears that the car may have been there since before Christmas.'

'And Unnur . . . Is there any . . . ?'

'At the moment there's nothing to suggest that Unnur was here,' Hulda said. 'But of course we're trying to find out if there's any chance she could have been.'

'Yes . . . OK . . . Can I ring you if . . . ?'

'You can get in touch via the police station here in the village. But rest assured that I'll let you know the moment I hear anything.' Hulda gave her the phone number.

'OK . . . OK . . . thanks.' The woman gave a shuddering sigh.

'Goodbye. I'll keep you posted.'

Hulda lay down in bed, closed her eyes and was immediately presented with the image of Dimma.

She could already tell that she wasn't going to sleep a wink tonight, and knew that she wasn't alone. On the other side of the country, Unnur's mother would also be lying awake through the dark, lonely hours.

XII

As she had feared, Hulda had hardly dropped off at all before she was woken by the phone on the bedside table in the early morning.

'Hulda.' It was Jens. 'I hope I didn't wake you. The thing is, they've found something rather odd behind the farmhouse. The rescue team came across a spade that had been covered by the snow. It looks as though some-one had been digging there.'

'What? Do we have any idea why?'

'No, we're working on it. Of course, the ground's fro-zen solid. But whoever was trying to dig there hadn't got very far.'

'Could someone have been planning to bury the bodies?' Hulda asked.

'Either that or trying to dig something up,' suggested the inspector. He sounded grave. 'I don't know if you remember, Hulda, but there was a heap of spades in one corner of the cellar, although the rest of the tools were neatly stowed away. It looked as if someone had grabbed a spade in a hurry and accidentally knocked the rest down.'

Hulda was silent. She couldn't get her head around this latest development. The full picture still eluded her, but it must become clearer, if only she could piece all this evidence together.

XIII

Unnur was sitting in her room in the attic. It was late and night had fallen outside; the darkness was depressingly quick to return at this time of year after being absent all summer. She was still labouring away on her book and, although she wasn't entirely sure that it was going in the direction she wanted, she reassured herself that she could always sort it out later. She had no intention of letting anyone read it yet, and anyway, there were only the two of them here. Erla's husband, Einar, was still away in Reykjavík.

'Anna,' Unnur heard Erla call from the sitting room. 'Anna, the coffee's ready.'

Unnur was a little disconcerted. Had a visitor arrived without her noticing?

'Anna?' Erla called again, a little louder.

Unnur got up from the table to go downstairs, but hesitated. Maybe she should just stay where she was and ignore this, because she could have sworn there was no one else in the house.

Erla called again: 'Anna, are you coming?'

Unnur left her room and went downstairs. When she reached the bottom step, she came face to face with Erla.

'*What were you doing up there?*' Erla asked with a puzzled smile. '*Why weren't you in your room?*' She was holding a cup of coffee and appeared perfectly normal.

Unnur felt a prickle of fear down her spine.

'*Erla . . . I . . .*'

'*Never mind, come and have some cake. Maybe we could play a game of cards? I've got a bottle of Coke in the fridge too. We should finish it up before your father gets home. It's not good for his waistline.*' Again, that smile.

XIV

Unnur had given up trying to break out of the room, temporarily, at least. She was terrified of Erla: there was a weird, unstable glint in her eyes that suggested she might be capable of anything. For some inexplicable reason, Erla kept calling her Anna and freaked out every time Unnur tried to explain to her that she didn't know who Anna was; her name was Unnur and she was just a girl from Gardabær doing a trip around Iceland.

And then one morning Unnur had woken up to hear the door of her room being locked from the outside.

'Anna, I can't let you leave,' Erla had said again and again.

Unnur was clinging to the hope that Einar would save her, assuming he actually existed. Until he got back, she reckoned it would be best to placate Erla. She was allowed to eat and go to the toilet, but Erla had taken to carrying a knife in order to force her back to her room before locking her in again.

It would be an understatement to say that this wasn't what Unnur had planned. Her adventure of a lifetime had turned into a horror film.

But Unnur was naturally resilient and had no intention of

letting this break her down. She had to stay strong. She wrote furiously and her novel was really getting somewhere. With innate optimism, she kept telling herself that everything would turn out all right in the end, but underneath, she was terrified. It had occurred to her to make a break for it next time Erla unlocked the door, but she couldn't be sure of getting away. The only way out of here was the road to the village, but that was too obvious and a tough farmer's wife like Erla might well be fit enough to catch up with her. It wasn't as if there were any neighbours within reach to turn to for help. Even though it was only autumn, the weather had turned grey and dismal, bringing day after day of relentless cold rain. She was in the middle of nowhere, and if she struck out into the surrounding wilderness, she was terrified of getting lost and dying of exposure.

She had decided, just to be on the safe side, to write a letter to her parents. She still had plenty of paper in her notebook and several envelopes in her bag, as she'd been intending to write to them regularly during her trip. Once she'd finished it, she put the letter in an envelope and hid it between the books on the shelf where she hoped Erla wouldn't find it. If her worst fears were realized, perhaps it would reach her parents one day . . .

XV

Hulda breakfasted at the guesthouse with her colleagues from Forensics, and Jens joined them, sipping black coffee while they ate. They sat there in silence for most of the meal, only occasionally commenting on some aspect of the case. Hulda had a strong suspicion of what they would find in the ground behind the farmhouse but wanted to avoid putting it into words, as if that way she could delay the inevitable.

'Well, isn't it about time we started making tracks?' Jens asked, without haste. It was already past eight, more than an hour since Hulda had been woken by his phone call. At that moment she heard the phone ringing in reception and had a sinking feeling that it might be for them.

She nodded, although she felt an extreme reluctance to return to the crime scene after learning of this latest development. 'Yes, I suppose we should get moving. Have they started the search for Haukur Leó yet?'

'I reckon they must have. No doubt they're still digging at the farmhouse as well.'

'Excuse me, Jens. Phone call for you,' said the owner of the guesthouse, who had crept up behind them without their noticing.

'For me?' Jens scraped his chair back noisily and got to his feet. Hulda remained seated but could hear the sound of his voice in reception.

He came almost straight back.

'They've found a body, behind the house,' he announced.

Hulda didn't say a word. She already knew what was coming next.

'They think it's the missing girl, Unnur.'

Hulda was hit by a wave of despair.

She had been staking everything on the hope that she could somehow save Unnur, though subconsciously she must have known all along that this was nothing but a fantasy. Yet, despite that, the news felt almost like a nightmare repeat of what had happened at Christmas.

Someone had murdered Unnur, Hulda was sure of it, but she had a hunch that whoever had done it had already paid the price.

When Hulda and Jens arrived at the farm, they learned that the initial examination of the girl's remains had uncovered evidence of injuries consistent with a violent death.

There had been no let-up in the snow and, if anything, the wind was even stronger, making it impossible to stand around outside for long.

The house seemed different in the morning light but, despite the cold, Hulda felt a deep reluctance to go back inside if she could possibly avoid it. She had been shown the remains and the shallow grave, the soil creating a dirty stain on the surrounding snow. The body had now been taken into the house to protect it from the elements.

So Unnur had been lying all these months in an unmarked grave, in a place where it would never in a million years have occurred to anyone to look for her.

Hulda wondered if she could have done anything different during the investigation last autumn. Were there stones she had failed to turn over that could have put her on the trail? Or had the whole thing been futile all along because the girl had already been dead by the time the inquiry began?

She reminded herself that there must have been some clue she had missed, though, since Unnur's father had found his way here.

How in God's name had he known?

Hulda wondered if he could have been involved somehow in her death. It was all she could think of at this stage.

'This just keeps getting worse and worse. I've never known anything like it,' Jens muttered as they thawed out in the police car. He sighed heavily. 'On my patch too.'

The doctor who had arrived with the ambulance had told them that, in his professional opinion, the girl couldn't possibly have died at the same time as the couple. Her death must have occurred weeks, if not months, earlier. They should be able to establish a more accurate time-frame after further analysis. For the moment, then, Hulda had ruled out a scenario in which Haukur Leó had murdered all three: Einar, Erla and his own daughter. The idea was absurd anyway since, logically, he must have come here *searching* for her.

Hulda also had to factor in the spade that had been found abandoned in the vegetable patch behind the house. Someone had plainly been trying unsuccessfully to dig there, but the spade alone would have made little impact on the frozen ground.

A story was slowly taking shape in her mind. Unnur, who had been planning to spend a year travelling around Iceland, must have stumbled upon this remote farm, with no suspicion of anything other than a pleasant stay. Hulda recalled what Inspector Jens had said about the couple sometimes taking in young people who worked in return for board and lodging. For some unknown reason, her visit had come to a tragic end.

'The poor girl,' Hulda said at last, after a long silence.

'He was looking for her, wasn't he? The man in the Mitsubishi. Looking for his daughter . . . ?'

Hulda nodded.

'And the result was a bloodbath.'

'Perhaps the couple refused to tell him where she was,' Hulda conjectured, 'or . . .' She trailed off, thinking, then went on, speaking more to herself than Jens: 'Perhaps they admitted that they'd killed his daughter and told him where she was . . . It's impossible to predict how some-one would react to news like that. You know, Jens, even perfectly ordinary people can . . . can lose control of themselves in extraordinary circumstances like that.'

XVI

'Erla, you've got to tell me what happened to her,' Leó said, and she could hear the fear and desperation in his voice.

Yet Erla was the one who ought to have been afraid, who was deeply afraid.

'What . . . what . . . ?' She couldn't seem to articulate the words, couldn't even shape a coherent thought in her head. The cursed mist that lay over her mind made it impossible to think straight.

'You know what I'm talking about, Erla. This has got to stop! I've got to find her! You must, you have to tell me, Erla!'

She just stood there, her body rigid. When he released his grip, she backed a few steps away but knew she was helpless, cornered like a caged animal.

'It . . . it spun out of control, do you understand?' Leó said. 'I never meant to . . . to hurt your husband.'

'He's dead,' she said tonelessly, and felt the tears trickling down her cheeks again. The words weren't really for Leó's benefit; she needed to say them aloud to remind herself that it had happened, to try to distinguish between reality and delusion. Einar was dead. That was real — she knew it now. And Anna . . . Anna . . . She *was dead too. It was as if a veil had been lifted and she could remember everything with a sudden clarity. The tears were for both of them.*

'Yes, but it was an accident, Erla. I didn't mean to hurt him. He had a knife and I was scared. The whole thing got out of hand. I was terrified he was going to stab me . . . I've never done anything like that in my life before but it was in self-defence, purely in self-defence . . .'

Erla nodded dully. Nothing would ever bring Anna and Einar back now.

She had to face up to the consequences of what she had done. Perhaps it would be best to answer the man's questions while she could, while her memory was clear . . . Because now, all of a sudden, she could recall everything that she had done her best to forget. Standing there in the dark cellar, she had no choice but to face up to the truth.

'Is it her you're looking for — Unnur?' she asked, her indecision suddenly gone.

'Yes, yes! For Christ's sake! I'm looking for my daughter. And you know where she is, don't you?'

'She came here, to work.'

'I know. She sent me a letter, but it didn't arrive until a couple of days ago. It must have been the letter your husband said he'd found and put in the post.'

Erla nodded and said: 'That's right. I didn't know about it. I had no idea . . .'

'What happened to her?'

'Einar never knew. There was no need to kill him.'

'It was an accident, I swear it!'

'And I didn't mean to hurt her, I —'

He grabbed her again, by the throat this time. She didn't resist, even when she felt his fingers tightening until she was gasping noisily for breath. In a weird way, she welcomed the pain. She didn't want to have to face up to anything any more . . .

'Erla, tell me, tell me! Is she alive?'

Her gaze met his, although she was close to losing consciousness. There was a gleam of hope in his eyes. He loosened his hold slightly.

But she extinguished it: 'No, she died. I'm sorry.'

His hands tightened again.

'I didn't want her to leave.' Erla was choking in his throttling grip. 'She was going to leave me, Leó. Again. Leave me again. My Anna.'

'What do you mean, Anna? Are you crazy? Why would you think Unnur was her?' He relaxed his grip again, enough for her to talk.

'Anna was my daughter,' she croaked. 'Unnur was sent to me because my Anna had gone. They were so alike. I kept getting confused and thinking Anna had come back – in fact, I was sure of it. I thought I'd been given another chance and it made me so happy, though I couldn't really understand what was happening. Einar was away, you see. And sometimes I can't cope with being alone here, I lose my grip on things . . . so I thought she was my Anna. But then she told me she was leaving . . .' Erla's voice cracked. When she continued, the words emerged in a thin, mewing sound: 'She was going to leave me again, but I couldn't lose her a second time. I refused to let her go.' She drew a gasping breath. 'It just happened. There was a struggle, I remember that, and then, somehow, she was dead. She died and left me again. I seem to remember there was some blood, but everything's so hazy . . . I threw her rucksack in the sea later, as soon as I got a chance. When I went to the village to borrow more books from the library . . .'

His fingers tightened convulsively again. Fighting for breath, she added, in a strangled voice: 'I knew you were looking for her. I sensed it when you arrived. Although I'd buried the whole thing. Couldn't bear to remember it . . .'

'Where's my daughter? How could you kill her? How could you?' Leó's voice broke and the last words came out guttural with tears: 'Where is she?'

'I buried her behind the house, in the vegetable garden. There was nothing else I could do. I had to stop Einar finding out.'

The deadly grip tightened round her throat again and she could feel her consciousness ebbing away.

She couldn't take any more.

XVII

Hulda saw a man she didn't recognize, in the orange uniform of the rescue team, come running through the thick haze of snowflakes towards the police vehicle. She nudged Jens, who hadn't noticed him, then opened the passenger door and stepped outside.

The man's voice sounded agitated when he could finally speak through his panting.

'We've . . .' He caught his breath and resumed: 'We've found him, or at least I think we have.'

The first thought to pass through Hulda's mind was: *How can I tell his wife? How can I tell her that we've found her husband and her daughter – that they're both dead?*

She dreaded the conversation so much that it briefly occurred to her to ask someone else to take care of it. She couldn't cope with any more tragedy or grief herself.

'Dead?' she asked, though it was obvious.

'What? Yes, of course – the body of a man. I'll take you there. It's not that far from the farm so we reckon he must have got lost and gone in the wrong direction.

Maybe walked in a circle. That's common when people are inexperienced.'

Jens had got out of the car as well.

'We'll follow you,' he said to the rescue team member, his voice unusually decisive.

Hulda stood, screwing up her eyes against the snow, intensely grateful that she was with the rescue team since, had she been alone, she would never have found her way back to the farmhouse. The air was thick with teeming white flakes in every direction. It would be frighteningly easy to get lost in conditions like this. No doubt that was how Haukur Leó had met his fate.

Alone in a blizzard, far from civilization.

Almost certainly with two murders on his conscience.

His body was lying in the snow, his backpack not far off.

Tragic as it was to think of his poor wife waiting at home, there was no getting away from the fact that if he'd lived, he would have found himself charged with double murder.

The man had been a virtual stranger to Hulda, though she had met him several times in connection with the investigation, at a difficult time in his and his wife's life. Yet she felt as if, on some deeper level, she had known him well. Staring at his lifeless body, she experienced a powerful surge of feeling. He had, in short succession, suffered an unspeakable tragedy, found himself caught up in these traumatic events, then lost his life without ever finding his daughter, though it appeared that he had suspected where her body was buried.

Even if he had murdered two people, she didn't get the feeling that this was the body of a cold-blooded killer.

Life wasn't that simple; the line between good and evil wasn't that well defined.

'There are two or three things we need to show you,' Hulda's colleague from Forensics told her. Haukur Leó's body had been removed and taken away for further examination, along with his rucksack. The police were now sitting in the dead couple's house. Evening had fallen, bringing a slight improvement in the weather; although the wind was still gusting strongly, the snow had at least stopped.

'We found a bloodstained knife in his backpack.' The man showed her the weapon, which was now sealed in a clear plastic bag.

'I suppose the chances are high that this was the knife used to kill Einar,' Hulda said.

'Well, of course, we need to carry out tests,' the man replied, 'but, between you and me, I think there can be no doubt, in the circumstances.'

Hulda nodded.

'He had a bunch of keys too, to this house.'

'And the third thing you mentioned?'

'Here.' He handed her another plastic evidence bag. 'There was this letter. I'm sure you'll find it enlightening.'

XVIII

Dearest Mum and Dad,

I'm so frightened. I wish I was at home with you.

This letter may never arrive, but I don't know how else to get a message to you. I'm going to hide it in here, between the books.

Hopefully, I'll be able to take it with me if I get out of here alive.

She's locked me in. Her name's Erla and she lives here. I'm in the east of the country. I'm enclosing the advertisement I found at the petrol station in Kirkubæjarklaustur, which includes information about how to find the farm. It's in the middle of nowhere, and the woman has lost her mind.

I'm locked in a room in the attic.

She keeps calling me Anna and won't let me leave. I don't know why. I haven't done anything to her.

I know you didn't want me to go on this trip and I regret not having listened to you now. I daren't try to escape, as she keeps threatening to kill me, saying she doesn't want to lose me.

Of course, I know you'll probably never see this letter, but I feel a little better just from writing it. I feel as if you're both so near and that somehow you'll save me.

XIX

Haukur Leó believed he'd found the most likely spot. Behind the house, under the snow, there appeared to be some kind of vegetable garden.

He had set out on this journey in search of his daughter, afraid he wouldn't find her but even more afraid that he would receive confirmation of her death. But he had to know the truth and so did his wife . . . They had talked of nothing else since Unnur disappeared but their desperate need to know what had happened.

They had assured each other that it was better to know the worst than to fear it, but now he wasn't sure they had been right. Now he knew, or believed he knew, that Unnur wasn't only dead but had been murdered, the knowledge was so horrifying that he couldn't think straight or work out what to do. It was as if the ground had been pulled out from under his feet, as if he had turned into a different person. He was a good person, or had been, but despair had changed him . . . When the letter arrived in the post, he hadn't been able to believe his eyes. He had been at home when it fell through the letterbox. He had started working from home more often because he found it so hard to be around other people at the office. When the letter from Unnur arrived, just before Christmas, it had seemed utterly unreal.

For an incredulous moment, he had believed Unnur was alive and the nightmare was over; that her disappearance had been deliberate and she was now writing to let them know she was safe. He had been about to leap to his feet and run to the phone to ring his wife at work when he saw the date on the letter.

Time had stood still. Feeling faint, robbed of all his strength, he hadn't been able to read any further at first, but when he did, he discovered that the letter was a cry for help. When she wrote it, though, Unnur had had no way of posting it.

It was plain that Unnur had been terrified. Haukur Leó had read and reread the letter, seized by an uncontrollable rage and hatred towards the woman called Erla. The letter had been dated early last autumn, not long after he and his wife had lost contact with their daughter. Since then, they'd had no further news of her.

He remembered Einar mentioning, carelessly, that he had posted a letter in the belief that it had been accidentally left behind by some boys who had been staying on the farm last summer. But it must have been Unnur's letter. It became clear to him that Einar had been innocent of any wrongdoing, completely unaware that Unnur had ever stayed in his house.

After reading the letter, Haukur Leó had made up his mind to go and find her. He hadn't even stopped to think. And now he knew that the decision had been a disastrous one. He should, of course, have gone straight to the police. Instead, he had got out his rucksack and packed his hunting knife, just to be on the safe side, as he didn't know what kind of reception he'd get, and a compass and some cash as well. His daughter had enclosed a leaflet with detailed directions for how to find the farm. Thus prepared, he had roared off in his

Mitsubishi, on the long, dark drive across Iceland, without a word to his wife. But then their relationship was increasingly character-ized by silences. They had so little to talk about these days.

Thinking back to it now, he wondered what on earth had come over him. Well, for one thing, he hadn't wanted to raise any false hopes in his wife and, for another, he had felt a burning desire to get even with the woman on the farm. He had been so angry. He still was. Full of a bitter rage. Words were inadequate to describe the intensity of his hatred. He no longer recognized himself.

The journey east had gone better than he could have hoped, in spite of the wintry weather. He had driven recklessly, breaking the speed limit the whole way, taking his life in his hands on the single-track road that unrolled before him, heading endlessly eastwards. Perhaps it would have been better if he had been pulled over by the police, since then he would have been forced to tell them where he was going and would no doubt have come to his senses.

But it was as if everything had conspired to speed him on his way. Hour after hour, fuelled by fury and hope, he had followed the rib-bon of road through the long winter night, across the empty wastes of the glacial plains, only occasionally passing the lights of remote farms, until finally he hit snowy weather in the east and was forced to slow his headlong pace. The morning was well advanced and a grey dawn had broken by the time he reached the turn-off. The road conditions, which had been reasonable up to now, worsened dramati-cally as soon as he left the Ring Road. Eventually, the way ahead became blocked with impassable drifts and, foolishly, he had tried to drive around them, only to get the car stuck. After that, there had been nothing for it but to continue on foot.

He was shocked by the force of the wind when he got out of the car, but he was well equipped and knew roughly how much further it was to the farm. All he had to do was follow the road markers. This proved easier said than done, however, since they were widely spaced and the wind was blowing up clouds of loose snow, almost as if the flakes were falling from the sky. If the weather had been any worse, he might have gone astray, but the luck that had brought him safely this far had held good. First, he had come upon another house. For a while, as it grew steadily nearer, he had believed it was the farm he was looking for, but once he got closer he saw that it was abandoned and realized that he hadn't walked nearly as far as he had thought. There had been no need to fake his exhaustion by the time he finally reached the farmhouse. It had appeared round a bend in the road, light streaming from its windows across the snow as if it were on a Christmas card, but he had known better. He knew that something appalling had happened there. The only thing he wasn't sure about was whether Unnur was still alive. That was the big question. So he had been forced to approach the occupants warily and try to scout out the place before revealing why he had come. Before the confrontation. In his haste, he had thoughtlessly given his correct name, his middle name, by which he was usually known. Presumably he'd got away with it, though, since his daughter's patronymic had been Hauksdóttir, not Leósdóttir.

The woman, Erla, had been suspicious from the start. No doubt the bloody bitch had guessed why he had come. She knew that sooner or later her monstrous crime would be exposed. She had kept a close eye on him, making it hard for him to search the house for clues. Nevertheless, he had managed, during the night, to sneak up to the attic, where he had found the room Unnur had presumably been staying in, only now there was nobody there. As he stood in the room, he had broken down in tears — he who never cried — because he had sensed then that she was dead. That he had come far too late.

He'd found it harder to figure out the man, Einar. Did he know what had happened to Unnur? And what exactly had happened in this house, which appeared so ordinary? It gave the impression of being cosy and welcoming, with the Christmas tree in the sitting room and the presents arranged underneath, the crackling hiss of the radio in the background; an old-fashioned Icelandic country home. The lies he told had been poorly thought out: he had got lost, yet no one was looking for him. He hadn't seen any other buildings . . . One foolish mistake after another. The moment he got a chance he had disconnected the phone in the sitting room, trying to do it as neatly and inconspicuously as he could. He had needed more time to assess the situation and hunt for evidence.

Then, somehow, the whole thing had spiralled.

Without warning, he had found himself in the same predicament as Unnur, locked up in the very same room as her. Perhaps Einar had known or suspected something and acted to protect his wife. Haukur Leó had tried to break down the door by brute force, but although he was much stronger than his daughter, he had failed. How must she have felt, being held prisoner here by a madwoman? His rage had intensified until Einar had entered the room holding his knife, and then things had turned violent. Haukur Leó had tried to wrestle the knife off him, afraid for his own life, and the tussle had ended in disaster, though he himself had been lucky enough to escape unharmed. He hadn't felt an ounce of remorse for Einar's fate. He had killed a man, but it had been in self-defence and, anyway, his own daughter had been killed while staying in this house. The whole thing had seemed so unreal: the blood, the body on the floor. Haukur Leó had stood there for a while, feeling oddly detached, and watched Einar's life ebbing away as he bled to death.

Then, coming to his senses, he had run downstairs to find Erla, only to discover that she had vanished. It had taken a good deal of trouble to hunt her down but, in the end, he had cornered her and heard her confession; listened as she described how she had senselessly killed his daughter. It had been the act of a deranged person. The girls had looked alike, his daughter and Erla's. It had been as simple as that. He had seen a photo in the spare room of a girl who presumably was, or had been, Anna. And it was true that there had been a resemblance; in fact, they had been strikingly similar, with that flaming red hair, and even a certain look about the eyes.

He had searched in the cellar for a heavy-duty spade and tried to dig, chipping and scraping at the hard-frozen ground. But to no avail. How long had he been out here?

He was so cold and exhausted he had completely lost track of time and had no thoughts left in his head now but to find Unnur. It was beginning to come home to him, though, that this wasn't going to work. He would either have to find another way, a more powerful tool, or get assistance. Perhaps simply call the police . . .

He had killed two people.

The first time it had been an accident, but the second time it had been cold-blooded murder; he had to face the fact. He had deliberately murdered the bloody bitch, squeezing her throat until she stopped breathing. And it had felt good. He had been avenging Unnur. But then, a few seconds later, he had woken up to the full horror of what he had done. There was no going back. Everything had changed. But now that he had lost Unnur, perhaps it didn't matter. He hadn't even decided whether to try and hide his crimes. They seemed of little importance in the great scheme of things. His daughter was dead.

It wasn't supposed to turn out like this.

He kept trying to scratch at the iron-hard ground, it was all he could think of to do, but he could barely even penetrate the snow to expose the soil underneath. It was like being in a nightmare, knowing she was buried under his feet but unable to get to her. He could hardly breathe. And all the while, the storm continued to scream around him. He was so cold and so deathly tired. But again and again, he felt a surge of new adrenaline coursing through his veins when he thought of Unnur lying there under the frozen earth. Even so, he couldn't go on like this much longer. He would have to rest, then make a decision about whether to seek help. Of course, he could fetch the police, confess to the killings and beg them to find his daughter. He was prepared to take the consequences himself but shuddered when he thought of the effect this would have on his wife. She would be alone, with Unnur dead and him in prison . . . Maybe he would get off, though; maybe the judge would take the mitigating circumstances into account and decide not to punish him. But even as he thought this he knew how implausible it was.

He stopped scraping with the spade and glanced up a moment. The gale lashed him with icy pellets and he could hardly see more than a few metres in any direction. He was trapped in a maelstrom of snow, alone, no one knew where he was, and he was at the end of his tether, both mentally and physically, crushed by the news of how his daughter had met her fate. And every now and then the thought surfaced that he was a murderer. Him! Though he'd been a perfectly ordinary person until his daughter went missing.

Perhaps he could go inside the house for a bit and recover his strength. But although he urgently needed a rest after more than forty-eight hours without sleep, he dreaded the thought of lying there brooding about Unnur and her fate, about Erla and Einar, the people he had killed. He had to find a way of completely emptying his mind. He just couldn't cope with it all.

He tried to carry on digging, then, overcome with a wave of exhaustion, he dropped the spade on the ground and set off back towards the house, telling himself he would return later and try again. He wasn't going to give up on his daughter.

The door was locked, but Erla must have had a key. He hurried down the steps to the cellar and stepped into the gloom. There she lay, just visible in the dim light that filtered from the doorway. The woman he had murdered. He felt his gorge rising and almost threw up but heaved a deep breath and concentrated on what he had to do – find the keys. There they were, in her pocket. He hurried out and up the icy steps again, round to the front door. His hands were so cold and weak that it took him a long time to wrestle with the lock, but at last he was in. When he entered the hall and then the sitting room, it was as if nothing had happened, with everything still ready for Christmas, as if no one had been killed, no one was lying in a pool of blood upstairs . . . Haukur Leó was overcome by dizziness and had to fight to stop himself fainting. The thought of the man in the attic was too much. He couldn't stay in this house, let alone sleep here.

He went to the spare room, where his rucksack was lying on the bed, its contents now strewn all over the floor. With trembling hands, he stuffed them back into the bag, then, snatching it up, he fled back outside.

It was like running into a wall. He stood stock still for a second, buffeted by the wind, blinded by the snow. It was too cold. No way could he go on digging in this. But he couldn't bear to go back inside the house either. He was so confused, his ability to think sapped by so many hours without sleep. What was he to do? He didn't know how to dig up his daughter, couldn't decide whether to confess the whole thing to the police and face the consequences. He couldn't think any more.

As if his legs had taken the decision for him, he started walking, head down, pushing against the storm, his only thought now to get back to his car. Once back in the Mitsubishi, he could gather his strength, warm himself up with the heater, then try to make a decision about what to do next.

He had found the way to the farmhouse when he arrived, so it stood to reason he ought to be able to find his way back. Or so he tried to convince himself, though the weather was far worse now. After all, the route had been fairly straight, with markers here and there to show the course of the road. Yes, he had no alternative.

He remembered more or less how far it had been to the next house and from there to his car. That should help him get a sense of how far he had gone. The most important thing was to keep going straight ahead, following the road that was buried in drifts somewhere beneath his feet.

Haukur Leó tramped along, keeping up as steady a pace as he could, aware that it was a long way and that he had to move briskly to keep warm. He mustn't give in to the cold. He believed he had enough energy left to see him through, if only he could stave off his fatigue for a little while longer.

He waded through the drifts, undaunted, refusing to give way before the battering gusts of wind. He had to keep his head down, couldn't look straight ahead because of the stinging snow, but he was on the right track, he was sure of it.

XX

Where was the abandoned house? He needed to find it to be sure that he was on the right road back to his car.

Had he passed it?

Was that possible?

Perhaps it was the blizzard, the poor visibility, that had caused him to miss it.

Haukur Leó had been walking for what felt like a long time and he was sure he should have reached the house by now. Yes, he must have missed it.

Come to think of it, he hadn't seen a marker for a while, but then he remembered that there had been a few gaps between them. He sensed instinctively that he was on the right track and that it wasn't far now to his car. He should be able to make it, though he couldn't deny that he was terribly cold and so tired he hardly had any strength left, as if he had used up his last reserves of energy.

But he had to make it to the car.

He was going to drive back to Reykjavík; yes, everything seemed clearer now. He was going to go home to his wife, sit her down and tell her the truth. She must be frantic with worry after the way he had vanished without a word before Christmas, like a complete fool. She deserved better.

He would break the news to her about Unnur; tell her what those vile people had done. His wife was a strong person; she wouldn't let it crush her. Then he would tell her how his journey to the east had ended: in the couple's deaths and the discovery that their daughter was buried in the garden behind the farmhouse. Then he would ask his wife what he should do. She would advise him to give himself up and he knew she would be right.

Erla and Einar were dead, yet he was still filled with a bitter, churning rage.

He was moving more slowly now, the adrenaline that had fuelled him to begin with was running out. Halting for a moment, he peered around, but the view was the same in every direction: a white wall. Finally, he acknowledged to himself that, for all he knew, he might have walked in a circle, because he hadn't a clue where he was.

There was nothing for it but to keep going and simply pray that he hadn't wandered off the road.

He had lost his sense of time; the truth was, he had no idea how long he had been walking. The whole thing was utterly hopeless. Should he maybe turn back? No, that wouldn't achieve anything as the snow must already have covered his tracks.

Perhaps the wisest plan would be to sit down and dig himself into a drift. Rest a little. Hope for a stroke of luck; an improvement in the weather, for example, though he knew this was unlikely.

Yes, that would be best. To bunker down in the snow.

He halted again and sank to the ground. It was a good feeling to be able to catch his breath and give his aching muscles a break.

He took off his backpack and laid it down in the snow, then

rested his head on it like a pillow. He wasn't going to let himself fall asleep, just relax for a few minutes.

He put his right hand over his jacket pocket where he kept Unnur's letter — he had to protect that.

Then he closed his eyes and his thoughts went homing to his daughter.

XXI

Hulda had found herself a seat at the back of the plane and was sitting alone, well away from the other passengers.

She was on her way home.

The noise was deafening but she tried not to let it get to her; she had to endure this flight in spite of the turbulence, the uncomfortable seat and the lukewarm coffee she was sipping carefully so she wouldn't spill it all over herself every time the plane lurched.

The coffee was disgusting, but then what could you expect on a plane? She had bought a newspaper at the airport to read on the way, but it had been a waste of money. She had hardly read a word because the moment she tried to focus on the print she started to feel sick, and the smell of the paper and ink, combined with the reek of fuel and the bitter coffee, made for a bad cocktail.

Yes, she was on her way home.

The trip had been an ordeal. The last thing she had needed was to find herself stuck with a bunch of strangers in unfamiliar surroundings in the depths of winter, trapped in the middle of a tragedy. As if she didn't have enough trouble at the moment, coping with her own grief.

She had been too quick to agree to take on the case, too quick to return to work. She hadn't got over it yet. No sooner had she formulated this thought than she regretted it, since of course she would *never* get over it.

She just had to learn to disguise her real feelings behind a façade, admitting no one, while at the same time behaving towards others as if nothing had happened, so she could carry on living her life – if you could call it a life.

She supposed the case had, insofar as it was possible, been solved. They would probably never establish exactly how Unnur had died, poor girl, though it wasn't hard to fill in the gaps now that they knew the background and had read the letter she had written her parents. The exact sequence of events that had resulted in the deaths of the couple from the farm was impossible to piece together too, though it seemed fairly clear that Haukur Leó had been responsible.

Four people had lost their lives and three of them had almost certainly been murdered, yet no one would be punished.

But then that's what her job was like at times, a game played out in the grey borderlands between day and night. No victory was ever sweet enough; her work was never really done. She could expect no praise or reward. The riddle had been solved to general indifference. Perhaps, though, that applied more to her, a woman in a man's world, than to her colleagues. She felt it so keenly, so repeatedly, the sense that some of her colleagues longed for her to make a mistake, to perform worse than them. It was the explanation for her deep need to prove herself, to constantly do better, but even that wasn't enough.

Yet small victories did bring her a degree of satisfaction. At least she herself could be proud of a job well done, even if no one else mentioned it.

This time, she felt nothing but emptiness, though she had performed her role well, in spite of her inability to concentrate. In fact, she doubted anyone else could have done better. But there was a void inside her that nothing could fill, like a hole in her soul.

She sat there on the bucking plane, gripping the cooling coffee, aware of the chill in her bones.

She was on her way home, but what awaited her there? Could she even call the house on Álftanes a home?

Not any more.

It might as well have collapsed into rubble on Christmas Day, when the family had splintered for good. Nevertheless, that's where she was heading, that's where she had to live, for the present at least. She had nowhere else to turn.

Of course, she could always knock on her mother's door, but she had no intention of doing that. Their relationship wasn't close enough, not on Hulda's side, anyway.

Hulda knew she would persevere with her job after this trip, although she wasn't in any fit state to do so. Jón was working from home a lot these days, even more than he used to, and she had to get away from him. At least when she was at work she could think, now and then, about something other than Dimma.

She could try to focus her mind on something she didn't care about so much. Perhaps her investigations would suffer as a result of her distracted state, regardless of the assurances she gave her bosses, but that was just tough. From now on, she was going to learn to put herself first. She had to get through this on her own. There was no other way. Jón provided no support, and she would never have accepted any from him. It was as if *he knew* that *she knew*, though neither of them said a word.

The silence between them was almost complete.

She assumed he would move out after an appropriate interval and vanish from her life. But even then, she wouldn't be free of him. There was still a risk she might bump into him in a small town like Reykjavík and, even if she didn't, she would know that he was at large, that he was alive, enjoying himself while Dimma lay dead in her grave. There was no justice in that.

Sometimes she considered screwing up her courage to bring charges against him. To go for it. Reveal the family's dirty laundry for all to see, put up with all the whispering that would ensue, about them, about her, wherever she went; malicious tongues asking – aloud – the same questions she kept asking herself over and over again: *Surely she must have known? Why didn't she do anything before it was too late?*

Why the hell couldn't Jón just face up to his own guilt?

Why couldn't the sick bastard just die? Do it as a favour to Hulda. Restore a little justice to the world. *Do one good deed in his miserable, worthless life.*

In the old days, she would have looked forward to her homecoming after a journey like this. There had been nothing to beat returning to the embrace of her family, in their cosy house by the sea, the sanctuary where she was spared the daily grind in the city. But those days were gone and, if she were honest, the feeling had faded long before Dimma took her own life. It had been a long, painful process, during which all warmth had seeped out of the house. Now, she couldn't wait for it to be sold. If Jón didn't take the initiative soon, she would put it on the market herself. She couldn't face walking past Dimma's room day in, day out. The moment of discovery had been so traumatic that all she wanted was to obliterate the memory, but nothing worked. Her mind kept conjuring up the scene, whether dreaming or awake, and Hulda knew that the moment would stay with her for as long as she lived. It was her last memory of her daughter, though she would have given anything to be able to concentrate on remembering the happy times instead.

She was on her way home to the cold. In her imagination, the house was now chilly and unwelcoming; grief shadowed her wherever she went in its rooms. She couldn't even derive the old enjoyment from going into the garden and gazing out to sea. Instead, she stayed indoors, lying in her bed all evening, sometimes cooking something when she was starving, but only for herself. Otherwise, she made do with having a hot midday meal in the canteen at work. She slept alone. Jón had moved into the spare room.

Hulda took another mouthful of cold aeroplane coffee.

The taste hadn't improved. Somehow, she must pluck up the courage to face the day ahead.

Try to soldier on, one day at a time.

Go on working. Do her best. After all, she couldn't sit idle.

She hadn't a clue whether she would succeed.

She was nearly forty. Where would she be in ten years' time? Or twenty, for that matter?

Would the memory of Dimma have faded at all by then?

And where would Jón be?

They would no longer be together, that was certain, but he was bound to have made himself comfortable somewhere else, perhaps with a new wife, having carefully buried the memory of what he had done.

Yes, *he* would be alive while Dimma was dead.

Then again, the bastard had a weak heart – though the doctors had told him it was nothing to be alarmed about, as long as he took his pills.

What a simple solution it would be if he stopped taking his medication. Yes, that would be best for all concerned.

And Hulda's spirits rose a little at this thought.

Author's note

I read books all year round, but I especially enjoy reading at Christmas time. It is an old Icelandic tradition to give books as Christmas presents, and then to spend Christmas Eve reading into the night. And books with a holiday setting are among my favourites. From the top of my head, I can name a few excellent examples such as Agatha Christie's *Hercule Poirot's Christmas* (1938), Ellery Queen's *The Finishing Stroke* (1958), Ngaio Marsh's *Tied up in Tinsel* (1972) and Simon Brett's *The Christmas Crimes at Puzzel Manor* (1991).

When I started writing crime fiction, I always knew I would want to write mysteries set around the holidays. The first such book was *Whiteout*, a part of my Dark Iceland series, and the second is *The Mist*. I have also written a few short stories set on Christmas Eve, one of which is published in this book for the first time, 'The Silence of the Falling Snow'.

For my Christmas writing I have of course been influenced by my own traditions, but also stories told by my family, one of which I want to share with you, a brief memory written by my mother, Katrín Guðjónsdóttir, a few years ago, a glimpse into Christmas in Iceland in 1960, when she was ten years old:

RAGNAR JÓNASSON

A Christmas with apples, 1960

It was a cosy feeling when Dad bought the Christmas apples, and the box was in our house in Háagerdi, in Reykjavík. Then I felt Christmas approaching.

We only had apples at Christmas time, so me and my sisters and brothers went, again and again, up to the top of the staircase to smell them. The box was open, but we only peeked; no one had an apple until Christmas Eve.

I always looked forward to having a bite of one as soon as I started reading a new book at Christmas.

I can still smell the apples . . .

Katrin Guðjónsdóttir